THE FACE OF EVIL

"The action and tension are constant, the fights very good, and most of the characters are nicely drawn… A very good book in the 'hard boiled tough guy' mold."

—Terry, *GoodReads*

"John MacPartland captures the loss of innocence, the yearning for something that never really was, the hope of redemption, and the cost of making a stand finally."

—David Vineyard, *Mystery*File*

"McPartland's best book is *The Face of Evil*, about the fixer Bill Oxford, who's been on the long downward slide of compromise, complicity, corruption, and has been sent to Long Beach by the PR agency to which he's attached to ruin a genuinely decent reform candidate, upon pain of being stripped of all his high-living perks and slammed into prison. It is tense and well-made throughout."

—John Frasier

JOHN MCPARTLAND BIBLIOGRAPHY
(1911-1959)

Novels:
Love Me Now (1952; reprinted in Australia as *Lethal Lady*, 1956)
Big Red's Daughter (1953)
Tokyo Doll (1953)
Affair in Tokyo (1954)
The Face of Evil (1954)
Danger for Breakfast (1956)
I'll See You in Hell (1956; also published in a pirated edition as *Run, Mann, Run* by James Keenan, 1975)
The Wild Party (1956)
No Down Payment (1957; filmed the same year)
Ripe Fruit (1958)
The Kingdom of Johnny Cool (1959; filmed as *Johnny Cool*, 1963)
The Last Night (1959)

Screenplays:
The Wild Party (1956, from the author's novel)
Street of Sinners (1957)
No Time to Be Young (1957; with Raphael Hayes, story by McPartland)
The Lost Missile (1958)

Short Stories:
Step Down to Terror (*Argosy*, Nov 1954)
The Night Is for Dying (*Adventure*, June 1955)
Party for the Kids (*Esquire*, September 1955)

Non-Fiction:
Sex in Our Changing World (1947)
For These Are the Bedeviled (*Esquire*, July 1950; article)

THE FACE OF EVIL

John McPartland

Black Gat Books • Eureka California

THE FACE OF EVIL

Published by Black Gat Books
A division of Stark House Press
1315 H Street
Eureka, CA 95501, USA
griffinskye3@sbcglobal.net
www.starkhousepress.com

ISBN: 979-8-88601-152-4

Text design by Mark Shepard, shepgraphics.com
Cover design by Jeff Vorzimmer, ¡caliente!design, Austin, Texas
Cover art by Ray Johnson

First Stark House Press/Black Gat Edition: July 2025

CHAPTER ONE

She was the kind of woman a man noticed, mostly because of her eyes. Dark, almost black pools, they had a warmth that I felt could turn to fire. She had turned her head, looking over the shoulder of the man she was with, and we looked at each other. The third or fourth time it happened he noticed it and I paid some attention to what he was like.

He was a type. You find guys like him driving ten-wheeler transport trucks, or flying, or sometimes as chief petty officers in the Navy, on a sub or a destroyer. Square-built, tough tanned skin, big hands with knuckles that are chunks of bone. The type — what makes him recognizable as a wanderer, a fighter, sometimes a killer — shows in his face. Big white teeth, yellow a little from cigarettes like his fingers, and he smiles with his teeth closed, talking through them when he's angry. A thin line of short black hairs for a mustache, sideburns of curling hair, hair black and curly, a face that is rough and yet young, and it won't change much if he lives to be fifty. The eyes are fierce, amused, hard.

It's a special breed of man, and the breed are men. Maybe a mixture of German, Irish, French-Canadian, with a strain of Comanche, Ute, or Cheyenne in there about three generations back. You meet men like this one in the truck-stop cafes along U.S.40, with the Diesels drumming outside; or you meet them walking toward the plane on the airstrip; or in jail, still smiling, still ready for a fight.

The guy was laughing as he swung off the bar stool.

He was still laughing as he walked over to me.

"You think my woman's real fine, don't you, buddy?" He was standing at my side, his feet wide apart, fists hanging easy, his leather jacket open.

There was more of that tight-curled hair at his throat and some of it showed below the cuffs of the jacket.

She was sitting on the bar stool, half swung around, looking at us. Dark eyes, glossy black hair, white teeth showing a little because she was smiling a little. I knew that she was curious as hell about what I'd do now; not with me, not against me, just curious.

"Gonna answer, buddy, or do I just take off on you?" The fists were still swinging loose and easy, the face was smiling, with the corners of the mouth too far back to make it a pleasant smile.

"Yeah, she's a fine woman," I said.

"Like to take her away from me?"

"Sure."

It was like a hand grenade going off in the little joint.

He'd be a one-two hitter, I'd figured, short left to the face, everything behind a right to the belly. He was standing. I was on a bar stool. I'd been thinking about these things before I'd answered him the first time.

My head hit his chest and came up under his chin as the left burned across the hair above my right ear. My elbow caught the right and I pushed him back and over, his knees coming up hard and hurting. My bar stool fell on us, we rolled, and he chopped at me with his left, three or four times, his fist jarring and solid.

The bartender was over the bar by then and he was no sissy. He had a sawed-off ball bat in his right hand, and with his left he grabbed the back of my collar and pulled me off, my collar tearing. The ball bat hit my body on the side of the head and the fight was over.

I stood up, shaking a little. My hand rubbed my face, the side of my head. No blood. The thing I was happy about right then was that I had my teeth. It would have been a teeth-on-the-floor fight, the way it had started.

The other man was pushing himself up from the floor with his hands, shaking his head slowly to clear it.

I looked across the angle of the bar to her. She was standing now; a small woman, with slender legs and slender arms, a simple, green-striped dress belted to show her narrow waist, full breasts, and small hips. She was a woman in a private hell — her deep-dark eyes and parted lips tormented with passion, with a held-in frenzy, with fear. And then it was gone, as if she could walk out of her hell, chin high, when she wished.

The bartender turned to look at her, and the other man was crouching, ready to jump into the fight again.

"All right, quiet down," she said to the bartender, "I'll take care of things." One hand touched the bar bat, and she held the other one out to the crouching man. "Stop it, King. I don't like it."

There was the bartender with his bat, there was the man, smiling again and ready, there were half a dozen people standing safely back, there was me — and all of us understood now that it was over. She had touched the bat and the bartender lowered it slowly. She had spoken to King and his smile was gone; he looked at her as if waiting for her to tell him what to do. I stood there and my hands went to my sides, the fingers opening. It was over because she wanted it to be over.

King stood up and her fingers touched his face as if she were about to kiss him. She shook her head as a girl teases a man with an unmeant refusal, and she smiled. “It’s all right, King. You made your point.”

She didn’t look at me again and he did only once. It was a strange look for a man like King. There was no fight, no laughter in it. I was startled. King had looked at me as if he were bewildered, uncertain, as if he needed help and understanding.

She slipped her arm under his and they walked out. We all watched them as they walked out of the bar, arm in arm. Then I bent over, righted my stool.

The bartender and I looked at each other. He let his breath out in a long sigh. “O.K., mister. He came up to you — you weren’t bothering him.”

What he meant was that it was all right for me to keep on being a customer. I sat down on my stool, the other customers drifted back to theirs, the red-faced man hiked up his apron and walked around back of the bar again.

I finished the rest of my shot. “I’ll try that again.”

“O.K.” He poured the shot, his thick wrist still shaking a little from excitement. I picked up the glass, held it for a second; the full brown-beaded whisky in the glass was like a small, quiet millpond. He got it. “You ain’t as hotheaded as you look, are you, mister?”

“Who was the guy?”

“Some guy. Fisherman, maybe. I don’t know. I’ve seen him around.”

This was Newport Beach, forty miles south of Los Angeles and a half-dozen different places all in one fairly small town. A fishermen’s town with a row of canneries where the big tuna are packed, and an end of the harbor full of the seagoing boats of the fishing fleet. A resort town for Los Angeles people during the summer. A tourist town for Easterners who can watch the white yachts on the other end of the bay from glass-and-redwood motels set in groves of banana trees. A sport fisherman's town, with only five miles or so between the fancy clubhouse bar and the moving seas where the marlin wait for the bait and the death fight. A piece of Beverly Hills squeezed together on Balboa Island in the harbor. And last, Newport Beach is a town where the lost ones try to live without being found.

The bar I was in was no fancy place. It was on the beach facing the sea, the long pier where families fished was a couple of hundred feet away, and the canneries were two blocks down. In the other direction a two-mile long sand spit led toward the resort section of Balboa and the ferry to Balboa Island. The sand spit, at its highest, was barely ten feet above mean high tide, but the Channel Islands on the horizon — Catalina and San Clemente — sheltered the coast here. Along the narrow sand peninsula were the motels, the summer homes, the House-and-Garden houses and gardens.

In the summer the two miles of beach would be cluttered with Mexican families down from Los Angeles and its more Latin suburbs, with children, with lovers, with tourists. This was early spring and the long beach was empty under a fog-gray sky. The summer homes were mostly empty, the tiny Coney Island of Balboa was closed, and the fanciest bars were shuttered. Two weeks from now they'd be closed again until summer.

But this was Thursday, a special Thursday. By tomorrow evening Newport Beach would be roaring on the beginning of a nine-day hurricane of young men and girls. Tomorrow evening Easter Week in Balboa would start, and right now something like ten thousand high-school kids and college students were getting ready for the one week in the year that was theirs. I knew what it would be like — and once you've seen the nine days in Balboa you will never forget them.

The bars would be filled with the most beautiful girls in Southern California. Not the shark-eyed girls of the studios and the television jungles, but kids from U.C.L.A., Southern California, Pepperdine, Oxy, and the rest. They'd be in fours, sixes, dozens, come down together to stay in a rented summer home, to have the nine days of spring. Those too young to drink would spend the days and much of the nights on the beach by the white yachts in the bay, or dancing to Kenton in the big barn of a ballroom on the ocean walk. They lived in swim suits, ten thousand boys and girls crowded into the winter ghost of a summer resort town for nine days of their own spring.

A smart woman anthropologist from New York had watched the nine days of Easter in Newport Beach and Balboa a couple of years back and she'd written a long study of it. She had called it a pagan fertility festival, as old as eggs and rabbits as symbols of spring; and with the same basic meaning. She had it about right, but it's no wild scramble of kids on the loose. The nine days mean something important to the kids, and they're changed during that time. It's impressive, awesome, and a little frightening.

"Another one?" The red-faced bartender had picked up my glass.

"Why not?" I was back in the bar, and it was still

Thursday, and anyway I was too old for the nine wonderful days that would begin tomorrow.

"That looked like it was going to be pretty good beef." Some guy had moved to the stool next to mine and was talking to me. I looked at him. A heavy man who looked as if he did heavy work, thick as an ox is thick, but with a friendly face. He looked all right to me.

I shrugged. The bartender put my drink in front of me and waited. I gave him a dollar and he mopped the bar a little before ringing up the fifty cents.

"Charlie here has plenty trouble with beefs. This joint seems to be a special place for guys to get hot at each other," the heavy man said. He was drinking beer. "None of my business, but what started that one?"

I took a drink. "He thought I was looking at his girl. He was right, too. She's got something."

"Do you know who she is?"

"Never saw her before."

"I don't know her, but I know who she is. That's Mrs. John Lisbon — Nile Lisbon. Her husband died a couple of years ago. He was one terrific guy."

"So?" I didn't want to talk about the woman. Matter of fact, I didn't want to talk about anything. It was a gray Thursday afternoon in Newport Beach, and I wished I was one of the five thousand guys coming down on Friday afternoon instead of being two thousand nights too old for the nine days of spring.

"Yeah, terrific guy," the heavy man said. "He was a lawyer. Best damn lawyer Orange County ever had. Straight and smart, that was John Lisbon. She's just as wonderful, this Nile Lisbon. Do you know what she is?"

"Good-looking woman."

"Yeah, she's that, but what I meant is that she's an assistant district attorney. That little woman — maybe twenty-eight or so — and an Assistant D.A."

"Still a widow?" Sure I wanted to talk about her, but I didn't want it to show. A woman in a bar with another man, and I'd been stupid enough already to get into a fight over her.

"Sure. After John Lisbon, what guy would stand a chance? You know, I bet that Charlie the bartender doesn't even know who she is. She never comes in joints like this — but everybody says she's a hell of a good sport. Hey, Charlie!"

The bartender came down from the other end of the battered bar.

"Yeah?"

"Do you know who that girl in the green dress was?"

The red-faced man shook his head.

"Kind of a girl that starts fights, that's all I know."

"That was Nile Lisbon, John Lisbon's widow."

"Her? That was Mrs. Lisbon?"

"Sure was." The heavy man turned to me to see if I was noticing the effect the name had. I noticed, all right.

"What was she doing in a joint like this? And with a guy like she was with?" The bartender was honestly curious.

"D.A. business, maybe. She wouldn't be with a guy like that on a date or anything. Not her. That's one woman that everybody in this town respects."

The bartender was old in the knowledge of the people on the other side of the scarred and butt-burned mahogany. He nodded and walked away.

"That's why I couldn't understand the beef," the heavy man said to me. "But she sure handled it neat, didn't she?"

"She did." I reached up and felt my torn collar. How fast a man can make an idiot out of himself! I thought. An hour in town and I get into something like that. I remembered the eyes. I remembered the brief look into her private hell — the passion, the fear, the half-opened lips. I remembered the smile when King had walked over to me, looking for trouble.

"You're still here. Good."

I swung around and looked into the night-black eyes. She was standing there, alone.

CHAPTER TWO

There was something uncertain about her smile, something eager in the way she looked at me, as if she weren't sure that she was welcome.

I stood up and smiled down at her.

"About that affair a little while ago," she said. "I came back to explain and to tell you I'm sorry it happened."

She came to my shoulder, the glossy black hair inches below my eyes. Her perfume had nothing of flowers about it, it was one of those scents that only dark-eyed women can wear, faint but vigorous, the scent of the musk glands of animals. Her shoulders were squarish, like a little man's, and her hand was on mine, warm, firm. I was looking into the depths of darkness in her eyes, but there was warmth there.

"You're lying," I said, almost with only my lips, a low, soft whisper.

She nodded, the smallest possible movement.

I held out my arm and we walked out of the bar

together. There was no need to turn around; they were all watching us.

The wind from the Pacific had wisps of spray in it; beyond the score of dinghies of the fishermen drawn up on the sand beside the long pier were the high rolling combers.

"I do foolish things." Her voice was surprising. It had an edge of strength to it, and it was clear as if she had been a singer.

"This one of them?"

"Coming back to you? Yes, of course."

"Another bar?"

"Maybe a nicer one."

"Christian's Hut?" It's a fake South Sea Island place in Balboa, but fake or not, it's one of the pleasantest bars in California, maybe in the world.

"They open today for Easter week — you know about that?"

I nodded and began to walk toward my car, parked by the sidewalk next to the stands where the fishermen's families sold the rock cod and such that their men caught, two miles out in a fog-locked ocean, working from an eighteen-foot boat with an outboard.

"Let's take my car," she said.

"Why?"

"If I'm in my car I have a certain freedom." Nile Lisbon had more than a certain freedom, she had a directness that matched the edge of strength in her voice.

I didn't say anything. Her car was about three down from mine, a smooth hard-top Buick, three years old. She opened the door, slid behind the wheel, opened the other for me.

"I've got a license," I said, not getting in.

"If you're proud you don't have to ride with me." No smile, no anger, friendly.

"I'll follow you in my car."

"That kind of man?"

I didn't answer. As I walked toward my car I looked across the street. The heavy man was outside the bar, watching us. I was thinking that the bartender knew more about women in general than the good people of Newport seemed to know about one woman in particular.

My car is a Mercury with some things changed around. The sport-car lads can call it a 'Detroit fat boy' if they want to; it has guts inside the fat body. I pulled out fast — there wasn't any traffic — and gunned it a little. I wanted to get to Christian's before she did. Kid stuff. There are only two streets along the two miles of low sand peninsula. She'd take the better one and I'd try the poorer one. About ten blocks to Christian's and a certain amount of risk from the Newport Beach police. I tried it along the single open lane of the divided street. When I got to Christian's she was in the parking lot, standing next to the Buick, talking to a young guy built like the stroke on a good crew.

She waved to me and I swung my car in next to hers. There were only two other cars in the lot. The tall kid with the shoulders and arms looked at me, started to say hello or something, realized he didn't know me, and just looked at me. Nile came over as I got out of my car.

"Hello." It was only one word, and she said it without trying for allure or even enthusiasm, but I knew I was glad to be with her.

We walked past the tall pilings in front of Christian's,

and up the stairs into the fake South Sea stuff — reeds, devil masks, shells, nets, and all the standard beachcomber stuff. They've got a record player somewhere, and a lot of soft 'Song of the Islands' music pervades the place, but very lightly. Two good things about the spot — the restaurant upstairs and the bar downstairs. The bar has a big window that you face, and the big window looks out on the fancy part of the harbor where the slim white yachts rock slowly, but the good thing about the bar is that it draws a pretty nice collection of people for a bar. At least, it had last summer.

We went into the bar, sat facing the tall spars and the white hulls on the gray waters of Newport Harbor.

"I'll have a bourbon and water," Nile said to me. I liked that; it's a nice little touch more women should learn.

"Bourbon and soda and bourbon and water," I told the barman, a sandy-haired young man in a crisp white jacket.

As he went to the other end she put her hand over mine, the same warm firmness again. There is a kind of woman that has to touch the man she's with. I wondered if Nile ...

"My name is Nile Lisbon. I live here." Her face, dark eyes, red lips, and all, was as politely serene as if I were the attorney for the defense on some case.

"Bill Oxford. I don't. They tell me you're an assistant D.A."

The fingers tightened briefly on my hand. She looked like a little girl caught doing something she shouldn't. Pale face, red lips, deep-black eyes, shining black hair — sometimes she had an exotic beauty, sometimes the mocking look of a bad little girl.

"Not a very good one." Then the mockery was gone and she was serious. "I work hard at trying to be a good one. Maybe sometime — "

The barman brought our drinks. We both lifted our glasses to click them together, as if we had always done it at bars.

"By the way, where's King?"

"King? Oh, King McCarthy. The man back there. I guess he had to go to work." Her voice had no interest. There is a kind of woman who can't remember the reality of any man except the one she's with. I wondered if Nile ...

"King was sort of annoyed with me." I said it for response, to try to find out something about Nile Lisbon, something important beyond the things I knew or had begun to guess at.

"Bill Oxford. It's a good name. Where's home, Bill?"

"New York, Chicago, Monterey. Different places."

"Married?" The fingers were tight again, but she didn't know it.

"No."

Her look had an odd intensity to it. Nile's face showed emotion so quickly, so completely, that being next to her was like being next to several quite different women. Now the dark eyes were watching me like those of a child who isn't certain whether the big people are lying to her or not.

"What's wrong with you?" The child look was gone; for the first time she looked the way she might to a man or woman in bad trouble, bad people in a jam with a woman district attorney asking questions.

I took a drink. "Because I'm not married?"

Nile shook her head. There was impatience in the gesture and I felt that one of the drives within her was to be understood, understood quickly, without explanations.

"Every man — every man I meet now, that is — has something wrong with him. Sometimes the man knows what it is. Do you?"

This was a woman that I'd fought over in a cheap bar, a woman who had come back to that bar to find me. She had gone to a fancier place with me, and now she was talking like this. Somehow I'd expected her to be different from other women, and she was. I'd expected this intensity.

"Maybe," I said slowly. "I'm selfish, for one thing."

She smiled; it was the bad-girl smile. "A man's supposed to be selfish and a woman isn't. A man and a woman do well together that way." Nile drank like a man, and the glass in front of her was empty.

"Any more questions, Nile?"

"Two more, Bill. What do you do? What did you think when I came back?"

I ordered another round and turned to her again. "I didn't expect you back. You were with a pretty good man and I didn't think you'd need another." It was a little brutal.

"It isn't that way with King at all," she said quickly. "I've got a man — or at least he has me — and I don't need any more. It wasn't that. I came back because I was sorry King was so hotheaded. You were looking at me, and I suppose I was looking back. King misunderstood."

"You're an actress," I said, turning to look into the dark pools. "You like to act. You're curious about men, and I think you like to make trouble for them. You'll notice I don't ask questions."

"You asked where King was." Nile took the drink

the bar man brought, raised it slightly toward me, then drank deeply. "You don't answer questions, either. Like the one about what you do."

While all this was going on I was completely aware of the charm, the whirlpool of Nile Lisbon. I felt an excitement in being close to her, talking to her. I wanted to stand up, take her out of Christian's, be with her. She knew it.

"You're an assistant D.A. in this county, among other things, so I'll tell you." As I spoke I looked away from her, past the devil masks to the darkening bay. A girl was standing on the deck of the nearer boat, a neat yawl. It was less than a hundred yards away. If the girl was wearing a swimsuit I couldn't see it. "I'm down here on business."

Nile waited for a moment and then she laughed. The complete change she could make so easily happened again. The beautiful woman, the child, the bad girl, the assistant D.A., all of these were gone now. She was just a friend, somebody you drank with and told jokes to, somebody you'd match for drinks. "O.K., Bill. If the cops pick you up, give me a call. I know all the bail-bond burglars."

The girl on the boat raised her arms. She wore her hair long, and in the last edge of sun over the hills beyond the bay her hair was a sudden golden-red blaze. Nile looked away from me, and saw the girl.

"I don't blame you, Bill. But I'm here and you'd have to swim for her."

"I'll call you on that," I said.

She opened her purse and took a cigarette from its case, and I lit it for her.

"Go for broke," she said, and she was talking to herself, not to me. She slid down from the stool. I stood next to her. A fairly big man, a small woman. This was a wild thing. We hadn't spoken a hundred words to each other, hadn't been together more than a few minutes, and yet I felt a possession of her as complete as if we were walking away from a marriage ceremony rather than a couple of stools in Christian's Hut. My fingers closed on her arm, tight and hard. I had to hurt her a little in that moment. She didn't flinch.

We didn't make it.

He had just walked to the doorway from the entrance as we reached it.

"Nile! I've been looking everywhere for you. I took a chance and came here, saw your car in the lot."

This one was tall, slightly graying, with the appearance of an honest judge or of the liberal candidate for Senator, the one who gets beat. Dark gray suit, fine shirt, quiet tie, soft, interested eyes, handsome in a dignified manner. I knew him.

I dropped my hand from Nile's arm. She stepped up to him and he put his arm on her shoulder. They were looking at each other and I felt as if the closeness I'd had with her a moment ago had been the casual politeness of strangers.

"This is Bill Oxford," Nile said. "Bill, this is Ringling Black."

We shook hands. He had a firm man-to-man grip.

"Have a drink?" I asked him. It was a curious moment to me, because this was the man who was the reason for my being in Newport Beach.

"Thanks, no, Bill. Nile and I'll have to run." He didn't know me; he was a natural first-name guy.

"Thanks for the drinks you did buy me, Bill," said Nile. She turned to hold out her hand to me and as I took it her lips formed a kiss that Black couldn't see.

For the second time in an hour or so I watched Nile Lisbon leave a bar with a man.

I went back to my stool. The deck of the yawl was empty.

"Another bourbon and soda," I said. In the course of a day I drank quite a bit of whisky. Why not?

"Yes, sir," said the barman. "That Mrs. Lisbon is sure a wonderful lady, isn't she?"

"That's what everybody tells me," I said, taking out another dollar. I was going to have to stop thinking about Nile Lisbon and start thinking about Ringling Black. I had a kind of dirty job to do on Ringling Black.

CHAPTER THREE

How does a man get to be wrong? This I don't know, except for one man — Bill Oxford. For me it was easy.

I sat there, alone now, and looked out on the gray-purple bay with the pale ghosts of ships in the twilight. This whisky I made last me a while. I can afford to drink as far as both money and the way I handle liquor are concerned, but Bill Oxford can't afford to be drunk.

The barman started to make a little conversation but I wanted to be alone for a while and think about things. Things like what I was in Newport Beach to do, and guys like Ringling Black, and exciting, probably worthless women like Nile Lisbon.

Wrong guy in a lot of people's books, this Bill Oxford.

"He'll cut your throat for a dirty dollar," they said about me, "and he'll look you in the eyes while he's cutting it." Which was about true. I didn't do it with a knife.

Once I'd been a newspaperman. Before that once I'd been seventeen and enlisted in my uncle's army. Fort Bragg when it broke open at Pearl, and I was with those wonderful kids from Bragg — Bill Bushemi, Jack Sher, Marion Hargrove — who were put on duty with *Yank*. *Yank* was a magazine, it sold for a nickel, and it was printed in different places like the CBI and the Pacific, the Persian Gulf and Italy, and a dozen more. *Yank* was honest and tough and fun. Sergeant Oxford was a fairly decent guy when he wore that shoulder patch; also Sergeant Oxford was kind of young when the war was wrapped up, and the honest, tough, funny sheet was wrapped up too.

There were jobs for the men from *Yank*. Bushemi didn't get one, he'd died as a combat photographer in the Pacific, but Oxford and the rest got them. My job was on a big, rich Los Angeles daily.

The paper had a city room full of hard-working newspapermen, and it had a few sharpshooters. The sharpshooters were the lads who got to the anything-goes parties in Bel Aire, and who got their places in line to try out the new models of star goddesses, junior grade. The sharpshooters were the boys who could run tabs on the Strip, and who took the yacht trips to Ensenada, La Paz, and Acapulco. Just knowing the right people and doing the right things for them. Kind of easy.

It wasn't *Yank*, this paper, and it wasn't honest or fun, but it was plenty tough. After a year the hard-working newspapermen were calling me "that son-of-a-bitch Oxford." They were right, but on the other hand I was getting some good Bel Aire parties, some choice young cutlet of starlet, some fancy tabs at Giro's and Mocambo that always got paid, somehow.

The front office liked it fine because the gentlemen that I was getting along so well with owned large oil-companies, large chunks of real estate, and large aircraft factories. A few of them owned large rackets.

You slide easy when you're twenty-something-early. You know a girl you've known fairly well, and you know some more people she's known fairly well, and so when a friend with a yacht asks if you know somebody, why, of course you know her and a few more like her. "Call Bill Oxford. He's a sharp kid and he can fix you up."

There's always a little trouble. Some lad from New York's midtown or Chicago decides to make himself a score for ten thousand or so with a touch of blackmail or extortion. "Call Bill Oxford. He'll handle it. The kid's tough and smart and he knows everybody." So they would call Bill and the blackmailer would end up with bad kidneys and no teeth, with nothing in anybody's newspaper and no ten thousand paid.

That's the way it goes. By the time you're twenty-six or so you've moved out of the city room and into a nice office in an advertising agency in the Hollingsworth Building, right on the forlorn corner of Hollywood and Vine. Bill Oxford the fixer.

The advertising agency, with its main office on Madison Avenue in New York, had some other title for me. The title didn't matter; I was the favor guy. Girls, parties, trouble, anything that was needed from Pebble Beach to La Jolla, turn the problem over to Bill Oxford. After a while I didn't have a real friend in the world.

A couple of years or so go by and you notice a few changes. The word has spread through town about you. You can get tramps for parties but you can't get the new, clear-eyed, hopeful, almost-on-the-level kids that you could once. Those kids know that you put the mark on them if they have anything much to do with you.

You've cleaned up enough smelly messes for important people so that you smell a little yourself. You aren't a real nice guest on a yacht any more because everybody wonders what mess you're working on for the guy that owns the yacht.

You've made a lot of gut-deep enemies. Some of them are women.

You couldn't write usual copy for a weekly newspaper in Lost Elk, Idaho.

You always need money.

You've lost something. Maybe you'll find what you lost at the Desert Inn in Las Vegas, maybe you'll find it at Sun Valley, maybe you'll find it at Charley Farrell's Racquet Club in Palm Springs. You know damn well you'll never find it again in your life, but you've got to run like a squirrel in a cage looking for it. Which makes you call the bank and ask them to hold those last three checks for a day or two.

But you get work. You've still got the office in the agency and people there still call you "Mr. Oxford" even if they wouldn't be seen having lunch with you. You're still the fixer if the job is dirty enough so that they have to use Bill Oxford.

That's how one guy got to be wrong. It seemed real simple at the time.

I drank the last of the highball.

"O.K., I'm ready to try it again," I said to the barman. The bay was black now, as black as Nile Lisbon's eyes. I decided to think about Ringling and how I'd fix his clock for the five thousand dollars it was worth to me.

The barman put the drink in front of me and she came in, the girl from the white-hulled yawl. I recognized the red-gold blaze of long hair and I could see that she hadn't been naked; she wore a short open coat over the same suit she'd had on on the boat. Something elastic and peach-colored.

She ordered a bottle of beer. The barman called her Joyce and didn't seem to know her too well in spite of the first name. Joyce was maybe a day or two over twenty-one. Where Nile Lisbon was exciting, and drew a man toward her like an invisible whirlpool, this girl was pretty and fresh, and probably a very nice kid.

Polishing the bar in front of me, the lad in the white jacket tried again. "Just visiting in town, sir?"

"For a few days." Whatever time it took to wreck Ringling Black.

"You'll be in for quite a time."

"Oh?"

"Easter week starts tomorrow. The whole town'll be full of kids. Real great."

Joyce spoke to me. "It's like Jimmy says — real great. A wonderful orchestra over at the Rendezvous, and some fine little combos in the smaller places. All the kids live in swimsuits for the whole time, and there are all sorts of parties — "

She ran down. I guess she realized that I was five or ten years too old for the wonderful parties or the dances every night at the Rendezvous. She didn't have to feel sorry for me. I'd been here once when everything was new and great.

What year had that been? Six, maybe seven back. Bill Oxford had fitted in O.K., sharp, but still a nice kid. Hell, it had been that Easter week in Balboa when I'd met Ann — wasn't it Ann? Yeah, sure, Ann.

Cute and trim as a palomino colt, that girl. Well, that's the way it goes for girls like Ann. I haven't seen her around for a couple of years, not along the Strip, or at any of the parties, or up for the big times at Del Monte Lodge. I guess it had got a little rough for Ann.

Joyce was looking at me.

"Didn't I see you out on the deck of that yawl a while ago?" I asked her.

She smiled. "I swim out to it almost every afternoon and take a sunbath on it. There's nobody using it until summer, it's anchored and closed up."

Jim, the lad in the spruce white coat, said. "The hull's all foul and rotten. The owners let it sit there for three-four years. Use it for wild parties in the summer. Too bad. It was one sweet boat, once."

I got up, left Jim a dollar, and walked out. It was time for me to go somewhere else. The whisky was getting a little hot in me. Another drink and I'd be trying to pick up the redheaded kid.

Outside it was cool and dark with a fresh wind from the bay. I left the car in the parking lot and walked toward the couple of blocks that were downtown Balboa.

Yesterday Mooney, vice-president in charge of the West Coast branch of the advertising agency, had called me into his office. Sleek, smooth Mooney came right to the point; he told me one of the big men wanted to see me, and right away. With Roger Mooney you say, "Sure, Roger," and jump through whatever hoops he's holding.

At least, they taught me to jump through the hoops. Do it nicely and you wear good clothes, live well, sleep with interesting company. Do it real nicely because there are always lads in the outer office anxious to show they can go through the hoop more gracefully than you.

The big man was a vice-president too, and his firm was a major client of the agency. They spent money for a fancy TV show that cost $30,000 each week, more money for full pages in color in the magazines, newspapers, and for billboards, even for a tame commentator on the radio. That money bought them extra services and I was the man who handled the extra services.

He was waiting for me in the gray-and-blond office beyond the reed-and-teak lobby that adjoined his personal secretary's office, which was reached by the private elevator in the big building on Spring Street in the deep-smog section of downtown Los Angeles.

"Hi, Oxford. Got a job for you." He didn't get up and he didn't shake hands.

"Sure." It could be setting up a party for him. It could be easing some used woman out of the trouble zone. Even something rougher, and this turned out to be.

"Primary coming up in a few days. We've got a candidate."

"Yes." The candidate's face leered at you from every third billboard in California. He was being built up as a fine fellow, but I wouldn't trust him in a graveyard, not if he knew where he could steal a shovel.

"We've also got a little trouble."

I waited.

"Fellow by the name of Ringling Black — an attorney down in Balboa has got some stuff on our man. Not good stuff by a country mile. Black intends to bring it out. We can't afford it, got too much money sunk in our man's campaign now, and if this stuff got out it would sink the son-of-a-bitch."

At least the candidate's supporters had him in the right slot.

"It would hurt us plenty too. We've been square in back of the bastard and everybody knows that we are. We'd look like crooks or damn fools if this stuff ever got out."

"Yes, sir!" I sang out, and his eyes narrowed at me across the big desk.

"This Black won't be bought. He hasn't scared. We've got to get him, quick. Understand?"

Again I waited.

"You go down to Balboa. Frame this Black. Frame him hard and fast. Maybe with a woman. Something like that, something plenty nasty. Do it before Sunday. You get a five-thousand-dollar bonus. That's all, Oxford."

I didn't say anything and I didn't get up.

"That's all, Oxford."

After a few years of the hoops they get to thinking they can talk to you like that.

"Maybe I'm not the man for the job," I said.

I saw his teeth, yellow and big under thin, bluish lips.

"You're the man, Oxford. You're smooth and smart, you know all the dirty angles. Just get down there fast and get this guy in a sling. I want to pay you the five thousand Monday morning."

I needed the five thousand like I need blood in my arteries.

"I've never framed a man in my life."

My voice didn't have the solid sound I wanted it to have.

"Then you've just started. Don't give me trouble,

Oxford. I'm damn busy."

I stood up now, looking at him. There seemed to be a dirty taste in my mouth, the taste of a six-year hangover, but not from liquor alone.

"Get this, Oxford. Sometimes we need a man like you. You're getting a reputation in this town as a smart fixer. We need this Black fixed. If you don't do it we'll find somebody that will. We've got to stop this Black cold and we will. You know that. But if you don't do it I'll have your skin. I'll smash you into a cell, and when you crawl out you'll crawl into a gutter. Can I do that?"

"You can." The simple truth.

"See me Monday."

"Yes."

I went out of the office and I don't suppose he thought of me again that day. He didn't have to. He was a big man and he had the power.

This was the first time it had ever been real dirty. But I knew that it wouldn't be the last real dirty job. There are plenty of jobs to do in Southern California for a smart, tough fixer whose soul has finally rotted away.

That's why I was in Balboa. I'd spent the drive down trying to fool myself, but I didn't fool so good on this one. This was a first time — and I could remember other first times back over six years. Ann was the first girl I'd brought to a party for somebody else.

Now I walked along the narrow street thinking about Ringling Black.

There's a little beer cafe in Balboa where the sport fishermen hang out. Not the rich boys from the clubs, but the fishing tramps who live for the pull of big marlin on light tackle in a gray sea on a day when they should be somewhere else earning a living.

I walked into the little place and King McCarthy was sitting on a stool. I took the empty one next to him.

"You still in town?" King spoke through his teeth, lips drawn back.

"You still hot?" I asked. If I had to I'd go some more, but there didn't seem to be much sense to it.

King sized me up with his eyes. These men, the kind like King, are pleasure fighters; barroom fights and street brawls are good fun to them. The trouble was that I knew he'd take me unless I got real dirty real quick.

"The hell with it," he said, smiling now with his teeth apart. "Have a beer. What's your name, rooster?"

"Oxford. Bill Oxford."

"King McCarthy." We shook hands. "I drive a semi for Silver Tuna Canneries. What do you do, rooster?"

This rooster thing was cold to me, but I let it lie. He maybe thought it was cool. "Just down for a visit. Nothing special."

All the place served was beer, so I had a beer on King McCarthy.

"This is a hell of a good town but it'll be filled with crazy kids tomorrow," King said. "Here's how."

"How." The beer tasted good. I was getting hungry.

"You'd never believe this guy and I were tangling the last time we saw each other would you?" King asked the bulky man behind the yellow pine bar.

The bulky man's eyes narrowed a little as he smiled and shook his head. The men behind the bars know King McCarthy's type, and they set the bat handle a little more convenient when they see the leather jacket, the jodhpur boots, the weather-used rough face with the hard, laughing eyes.

"I was with a lady, one damn nice lady, down at Tug's joint in Newport. I got the idea this rooster was looking at her too close. You were, weren't you?" King was smiling at me.

"That's right." I was smiling too.

"So we went round until Tug's man tapped me with his club. By the time my head got right again, the lady was asking me to be a good boy, and you know King — whatever a lady asks for she gets."

"Not to be personal," I said, "but what happened to the lady?"

King laughed, big and loud. "Not to be personal, you hot hunting son-of-a-bitch! She had an appointment, a business appointment."

The interesting thing about drinking with King, not only for me but for any man, is that it was a lot better than six, two, and even to end in a fight. We'd talk and drink and laugh and call each other names, still laughing, and then somebody's fist would hit somebody's jaw, and somebody would kick somebody else's teeth out. Interesting as hell.

"She came back to the bar to see me," I said. "Her name's Nile Lisbon and we seem to like each other real fine." When he moved he'd get the beer in his eyes, and then I figured to get his open jacket down over his shoulders while I gave him the knee. Maybe it wouldn't work but that's the way I was figuring the action.

Nothing happened.

"Yeah, I guess that's what she did," King said slowly.

I didn't say anything. Out of the side of my eye I could see the bartender close to us, his right hand under the plank of the bar. If there was going to be action I'd change my plans and let King get the first one across, then it would be his head that got the bat again. Fisherman's town, probably used up a lot of bats every year.

"I can't figure her at all," said King, and he was looking at me with the same odd look he'd had back in Tug's place when he left — bewildered, uncertain. You don't see that look on the faces of men like King often, and when you do it's betting a cinch that a woman put it there.

"We talked for a while. Then a man named Ringling Black found her."

"Yeah. Mr. Black. He wants to marry her. He was her husband's law partner."

"Seemed like a nice guy." The tension was over.

"He's a swell guy. Not as swell as John Lisbon, but plenty O.K. John Lisbon was the best guy that ever lived. He was my lawyer. I used to get in trouble — you know, drunk, or maybe a beef, or my ex-wife trying to get me in a wringer. John Lisbon would handle it, fair and square."

The bulky bartender had both of his big square hands on the bar now. He knew the storm had blown by. "Best guy that every lived in Orange County," he agreed.

"You know there's nothing between Mrs. Lisbon and me," King said, looking at me. "Not a damn thing except we're friends. Sometimes she gets tired of everything and she calls me and we have a few drinks together and that's it. You understand?"

This time I knew how to start a fight for certain. All I had to do was tell him I didn't believe him and the war would be on.

"Sure I understand," I said. "What's with this

Ringling Black? He's got offices here in town, hasn't he?" Get to work, Bill Oxford, get down to your dirty five thousand bucks' worth of work.

The bulky man nodded, picking up a bar rag. "Right down at the corner in the new building. He handles a lot of wills, estates, stuff like that. He's in politics, a little bit. Kind of a liberal, but he's never run for anything."

"Give us a couple more beers," I said.

"Not for me. I gotta get in the rig pretty soon and take it north to San Luis. Due at the warehouse there by midnight." King got up, put out his hand again. "Glad to meet you again. You understand about Mrs. Lisbon?"

"Completely," I said. I didn't understand anything about her, and particularly I didn't understand the fascination the dark woman had for everybody, including me.

King McCarthy and I shook again and he left. He'd spend the evening behind the wheel of a big Diesel truck and semitrailer, hauling cans of tuna north to San Luis Obispo. I would have traded jobs with him very happily.

The three other men in the place, the bulky bartender and I talked marlin fishing for about three bottles of beer's worth of time. Then we talked about the town and some of the people. Ringling Black for one. All of them knew him, all of them liked him. The only time he got the worst of it was when they compared him with John Lisbon. That brought in the widow, Nile Lisbon.

Besides being fishermen, these were four of the lads. They were all in their late twenties or early thirties, with the lean, tough muscles that seamen have but with the twist of the mouth that a man gets when he knows too many people too well. There are a lot of sportsmen's wives in the area during the season, a lot of young chicks, a lot of this and that. These boys got their share of all of it.

They thought Nile Lisbon was a fine girl.

An hour or so ago she had said to herself. "Go for broke," and had started out of Christian's with a man she had just picked up. The last I'd seen of her was her red mouth dry-running a kiss to me while her back was toward Ringling Black.

"She's too nice to be an assistant district attorney," said the man behind the bar. "She doesn't know about all the stuff that goes on."

I paid for the beer and moved on.

The Balboa end of Newport Beach isn't big. A score of motels, three fancy bars, a couple not so fancy, a big dance hall, dark now, on the ocean side, a few stores. On the ocean side is another pier, like the one in Newport; on the bay side is a casino, with the sport-fishing boats anchored or docked around it. There's one big gambling joint in town, run quiet but high. It handles around ten thousand a day in horse bets alone, and there are a few games too. Newport Beach uses the tricky California law that makes draw poker legal, and it's always been a fastmoving town.

When the fishermen come back up from the waters off Baja California or clear from Panama with the seiners' big holds loaded gunwale-down with albacore, or come back from Ketchikan and the Alaskan waters with the four-and five-figure cannery checks in the strongboxes, they're ready for action in Newport. With civic pride Newport tries to give it to them, as fast, as hard, as quiet, and as rough as possible.

I walked into the big joint. A lot of sets of eyes turned and looked over the stranger. One man, bald and broad, came over to me.

"Good evening friend," he said.

"Some action. Draw. Table stakes."

He kind of sighed a little. I was probably one of two kinds of guy, he was thinking: a real ripe one, just as good as a check for the next month's rent for the place, or I was a stupid sharpie, planning on chiseling. He didn't care; in a little while he'd know.

"Sorry, friend. No table stakes, but we've got an interesting table over here with a seat that happens to be open."

"Twenty limit?"

"Ten, but friend, you know even ten makes a very interesting game."

Sure, you can drop a thousand in half an hour, I thought.

I dropped a hundred. Same old game — two house shills cross-raising when it was worth doing, three other players who worked with the cards glued to their bellies. Table stakes and my four hundred or so would have made for a little excitement, but the limit game was about as much fun as a rigged slot machine.

You know what's the matter, Bill Oxford, I thought when I was out in the cool blackness again. You want to be with Nile Lisbon. Why, God knows. You hate to start work on Ringling Black because when you do it's the end of the last trace of the good kid who used to work on *Yank*.

I stopped at the Inn and picked up the room I'd reserved by phone. Then back to Christian's Hut for a steak, looking through the glass wall at the lights shimmering in the waters by the bay.

Downstairs for a drink at the bar. It was crowded now, and there was the laughter of women, the low voices of men. A good bunch — the women all beautiful or close to it, the men rich-man brown and with good clothes.

Joyce was still there, a little high, still in the short coat and bathing suit, her blaze of hair shining. She was with the kind of guy she should be with now, the longhaired young lad from the parking lot. She remembered me enough to wave a hello with a smile, and the broad-shouldered kid looked at me the same way he had in the parking lot, starting to smile and then just looking.

I sat down and ordered bourbon straight.

"You son-of-a-bitch. I'm glad I found you. I'm going to kill you, and that's too good for you." The voice was a woman's, low, close to my ear.

When I turned around I saw Ann. She didn't look too good.

CHAPTER FOUR

Ann, who had looked rangy and golden like a palomino colt; even at twenty-two she'd had the wide-eyed laughter of a youngster to whom the world was new and good. That had been six years ago, during Easter week, here in Balboa.

Now she was sleek, a jungle animal who'd been caught and caged in a filthy zoo too long, the kind of girl who describes herself as a model but who does no modeling. Her eyes weren't wide, nor was the world new and good to her. Any man could see all that. I could, better than any other man.

"Hello, Ann."

"Don't hello me, you son-of-a-bitch. I'll kill you and spit on your corpse."

She was drunk. I got up, put her on my stool. The sandy-haired lad in the white jacket behind the bar raised his eyebrows. To bartenders girls like Ann meant trouble.

"What have you been doing, Ann?"

Her still lovely face was sullen. "Doing the best I can."

"Drink?"

"Sure you can buy me a drink, you dirty scum."

"Is it still Dubonnet?"

She laughed. "Gibson. That's all I drink, Gibsons." The laugh would have been nice if there'd been any humor in it. The Gibson is the mean big brother of the Martini, devised for people who won't ask for straight gin but want it.

"Gibson, bourbon straight, soda back," I told the barman. His lips were tight in disapproval. Apparently Ann was known to him, and not pleasantly. But the place had been closed since last season, and had opened today only for the nine days of spring. If she had done anything, it had been tonight.

He put the two drinks in front of Ann. I was standing behind her, she was staring straight ahead.

Ann Field. Her folks used to have a few acres of oranges near El Toro marine flying base and they had been strict with her. That story. At twenty-two she was already a little old for the sap-deep excitement of Balboa when it belongs to youth for nine vernal days. I met her and thought she was a lot of fun, but I was teamed with a redhead, like this Joyce, that year. Yet Ann was always around, and there was a party up at a big place near Malibu, so I asked her up, but not for me.

Maybe nothing happened that time. But another friend was taking a party down to La Paz at the tip of Baja California for marlin fishing and hell generally. I asked her if she wanted to go, and she did. I didn't make the trip myself. After that I used to see her around, but she didn't have much to do with me. Then after a few years I didn't see her around any more, but then, girls are always sliding away and new girls take their places.

The hell of it was that when I did it, six years ago, I didn't realize what I was doing. The real hell of it is that I know it now.

"How are the folks, Ann?"

"The orange grove went bust a couple of years back. They're in Los Angeles in some stinking little hotel. What's it to you, you lousy scum?"

"Why so hot at me, girl?"

"Because I hate your rotting guts. Next question."

"Why?"

She turned slowly and looked at me. The people on each side of her were listening. It didn't bother me. I've been called worse names in public in the last few seasons. In fact, I don't like strangers to think well of me, because after a while they might get to be acquaintances.

"You don't know why I hate you and why I'm going to kill you?"

"Go ahead, tell me."

"Because I was crazy in love with you once. You were the greatest guy in the world to me. I knew that damn redhead wouldn't last, and I knew that you and I would get married and have kids and life would be one goddamn wonderful dream."

"Not from me you didn't know those things."

She said a couple of nasty words. The woman on her left turned away, but I suppose she kept on listening.

"So you invite me to a party. I was the happiest goddamn girl in California. Only you weren't my date."

"I told you that." This was futile. These were ghosts of six years ago.

"Yeah. Then you put me on a boat, with a lot of old men and a lot of liquor. I suppose you didn't know what was going to happen?"

I didn't say anything. The woman on Ann's left and the man on her right both turned to take a look at me.

"Why didn't you tell me all this before, Ann?"

"I never was drunk enough to tell you."

"What can I do now?"

She took a long drink of the water-clear Gibson.

"What are you down here for? Looking for young kids during Easter week?" She had turned back to the bar and spoke over her shoulder.

"No, I'm down here on business."

"I'll bet it's dirty business."

I finished off the shot. "So long, Ann. I'm sorry."

"You're not leaving me, you dirty scum." Her voice was still low, but she slid down from the stool and her right hand grabbed my jacket sleeve.

"O.K., Ann. Come along."

We walked out together. She was staggering and held on to me to keep from falling. Well, they knew me real good at Christian's Hut now.

Outside, standing in the darkness, I asked her. "Where are you staying?"

"No place. I came down here on a bus this afternoon

and I've been getting tanked ever since. Mr. and Mrs. John Jones of Seattle broke up their marriage in a hotel on Santa Monica Boulevard this morning. Mr. Jones didn't know about it because he hadn't waked up to his hangover yet. Any more questions?"

"No, Ann. No more questions. Yes, one more. Would you take a loan from me?"

"I told you, I'm going to kill you."

She was in bad shape. I led her to my car, helped her in. Then I got behind the wheel. She slumped against me. I pulled out of Christian's lot, drove up to the long street, and turned left. There was a motel a couple of blocks down. I went into the office and registered for a single for Ann Fields. I put down a license number, somebody's I guess, but not mine, and paid fifteen dollars.

"You can have it for tonight only," said the elderly man who took my registration. "We're all filled up with kids for the next nine days. Easter week."

"Yeah."

I took the key, drove the car to the cabin, opened the door, and carried Ann inside. I put her on the bed and started to walk out.

"Just remember I'm going to kill you, you lousy son-of-a-bitch," she said, clear and soft. I closed the door with the key on the inside. Then I drove back to Christian's Hut. They might as well know there that it didn't end in either death or love for me tonight, as far as the drunken, evil-talking blonde was concerned.

The stool Ann had been on was still empty, but the crowd hadn't changed much. My friends to my right and left recognized me. The woman smiled. I didn't smile back at her.

There were two additions to the crowd that I didn't

notice until I had my first drink. Nile Lisbon and Ringling Black were at the far end. I took my drink and walked over to them. I was hungry to be close to Nile Lisbon again.

If she was an actress, she was a good one. She saw me, and her head tilted back, eyes suddenly big, lips parted, as if something exciting had suddenly happened to her.

Black probably was annoyed to have any man break in on them, but he was too much of a gentleman to show it. He remembered me, remembered my name, and he smiled a welcome. Nile hid the look of excitement, smiled as at an acquaintance.

"Bill Oxford! Why don't you join us?" Black said.

I could have told him that being a gentleman is sometimes foolish and expensive. Instead I said, "Happy to. Why don't we go in the other room and get a table?"

He didn't like the idea but he still had to be the gentleman, smile, and say, "Good idea."

Nile Lisbon looked at me, her eyes deep and black, her lips open to blow out a long plume of cigarette smoke. Her face was without expression. The three of us went into the other room, found a small table. A few flames were flickering around a bed of glowing coals in a circular hooded fireplace in the center of the room. A waiter bobbed up and took our order from Black. Three highballs.

"Finding Newport interesting?" asked Nile.

"I was here a few minutes ago. I didn't see you then."

"We've been making the town," Black said. "Vaux's, the Park over on the Island, and a little place in Newport that I'd never been to before. Rather an honest place, fishermen mostly."

"Tug's, by any chance?"

"You've got me. I didn't notice the name."

"It was Tug's," said Nile. While she spoke her voice was oddly lifeless, but then she turned to me, the tip of her tongue barely showing between smiling lips.

"I feel almost useless in a place like that," Black said, "with men who earn their living in a basic way, not like a parasite of a lawyer."

"Tug's is quite a place. I like it myself," I said. It was like looking at a schedule: Nile and I would sit here drinking patiently until Ringling Black had to go upstairs, and then we'd make some kind of date for tonight. I knew it, and she knew it. We didn't even look at each other for a long time.

This was the man I had come to Newport to frame. There are only a few ways you frame a man — money, women, liquor. There are others, but they aren't so useful. I watched Ringling Black drink and I could see he was no lush.

Of course it's been done before — slugging a man's last drink with something that will hit about the time his car is in the stream of traffic. Even in my own sorry code of good and bad, that was out.

Money. I'd had a careful run-down on Ringling Black before I left Los Angeles. The big men behind the candidate had checked out Black with private detectives, accountants, and a combing of the records back to his birth certificate. He was clean. Inherited some orange properties from his family, earned some $20,000 a year beyond that. Partner of John Lisbon, now senior partner to a local young lawyer with good social connections, Jay Packard. Ringling Black was as honest as the multiplication tables.

Now I was listening to him in a small conversation

over the table. He talked like a man who is a gentleman solid through to the core. Nile was good company, a girl who could laugh easily, listen well, and tell quick, pointed jokes. After the years I'd had, all I needed to do was push some button in my mind for the right level of talk and jokes, turn on the automatic variable smile, and go back to my own thoughts. I didn't even have to listen to my own stuff; it was a taped job.

It would have to be a woman. I needed that five thousand dollars. I owed nearly that much back in town. If I didn't get it, I was in a box. Within a month there'd be no more office in the Hollingsworth Building, no more "Mr. Oxford." No more house up in Benedict Canyon. No more souped-up Mercury. I've seen all that happen to other sharpshooters like Bill Oxford. It takes six months to two years until they've disappeared completely or until they're on the muscatel beat along East Fifth in Los Angeles.

Sometimes, for cruelty and a curious turning of the knife in our own guts, we'd go down to East Fifth at night. They'd be there, four or five men we'd known a few years back when they'd had their Jaguars and their women and their houses on the tops of the hills. Now they would be wino bums, filthy, stupid with muscatel or white port, dead men shuffling through the wreckage of East Fifth. They wouldn't know us.

I had to have the five thousand. Besides, you don't go back to the big men with excuses. You take the job, you do it neatly, and you get paid.

Nile was no girl to play footsie under the table, no girl to play games with her eyes across the table. I began to wonder when Ringling Black would have to go upstairs. It was a little after eleven.

I took a long look at Nile Lisbon, trying to find the secret of the whirlpool that I could feel even now. Dark eyes, pale face, shining black hair, red lips, good body — and something more. There was an animal there, fierce, frantic, frightened, dangerous.

Ringling Black saw the look and the conversation stopped for a moment. He wanted to marry Nile Lisbon. Why not? Why didn't it happen?

It would have to be a woman, I thought to myself, and it would have to be quick. Ringling Black was getting ready to spring his trap on the big men's candidate, bring out his solid proof that the guy was a crook and a vicious pervert.

What woman would I use? I thought about Ann Field. Nile Lisbon.

You've seen a rat in a box.

CHAPTER FIVE

"Excuse me for a moment," said Ringling Black, standing up. I nodded, Nile smiled. I watched his broad, straight back in the well-tailored dark suit, saw him turn to go upstairs to the men's room.

"Where and when?" I asked Nile.

"You're damned sure, aren't you?"

"Yes."

"Maybe it could be you. I thought it could be you when I saw you in Tug's with King walking toward you for trouble. Maybe it is you." Her voice was low, almost a whisper, and there was pain in it, pain that showed on her face. For just a moment her hand was on my wrist.

"On the bay front, the two-story stone house. The

door will be open."

"I'll be there."

Ringling was coming down the stairs.

I waited until he reached the table, then I got up, bowed to Nile, shook hands with him, and left them.

Outside the moon was riding above a thin, low fog. I got in my car, drove to the bay front where Newport harbor narrows to meet the ocean beyond two long stone jetties. The two-story house was there, almost the last house in the row of big homes. It was dark. Eleven-thirty now. Maybe about two-thirty. Three hours.

Somehow taking the girl he was in love with seemed right. If I had to do this other thing to him, I might as well give him the full treatment.

I swung back along the bay to where the ferry slip is, halfway between the casino and Christian's Hut. Three other cars were waiting for the scow-shaped little ferry to chug from Balboa Island, maybe three hundred yards or so across the main channel of the harbor.

The ferry nudged against the pilings, the ramp was lowered to its deck, a couple of cars rolled up, and the four waiting cars came down. The ferry held three, and so I braked to stop at the head of the ramp. Five minutes' wait while the ferry made its round trip. Five minutes more cut out of two hours. I laughed at myself, nervous and impatient as a high-school buck waiting for his first date with the girl that the older guys have been whispering about. That's how I felt.

"Hello, chiseler." A man was standing beside my car looking at me.

"Who the hell are you?" I had no doubt that it was someone who knew me, but I didn't recognize him.

Ordinary height, ordinary build, ordinary face, as much as I could see in the single light over the ferry slip.

"You're Bill Oxford. You're down here to do the dirty to Ringling Black. Right?"

"Get in," I said. I didn't know the guy, but he sure knew me. He walked around the front of the car and I opened the door for him.

"Tell me about yourself," I said.

"You came into Newport this afternoon, parked your car near the pier, went into a salon called Tug's, got into a fight with a truck driver named King McCarthy, stayed there. A woman named Nile Lisbon, an assistant district attorney in this county, came back to see you. The two of you went to Christian's Hut. She left with Ringling Black. You went to the Kitchen, met McCarthy again, didn't fight with him. You went over to a card room that fronts for the big bookie here, dropped five twenties in the draw game, went back to Christian's, had steak for dinner, went to the bar, met a girl named Ann, took her to a motel, registered her under the name Ann Field and a false license. Then you returned to Christian's, met Ringling Black and Nile Lisbon. You drank with them for some time, drove to Nile Lisbon's home, looked at it, and came here."

"I'll be a son-of-a-bitch," I said.

"You are," he said. "But then, so am I."

I reached over, took his left hand in my right, my hand pressing down on this thumb, and pushed the heel of my left hand under his chin. I twisted his hand and shoved his head back over the edge of the front seat, swinging my body so that my left knee came out from under the wheel and over into his stomach, then I dropped his left hand and hit him below the ear.

Cop's trick — except for the punch.

If I hadn't been nervous over Nile, I might not have been so quick to be rough. There were a lot of things churning in me — the job, the money I had to have, fear, disgust, Ann, a strange blind restlessness just from being in Balboa as the nine days of spring were starting. It was no time for a stranger to be cute with me.

He hadn't made a sound. I let my left hand ease down until his head was straight. He shook it, rubbed his jaw with his right hand.

"I've been slugged before," he mumbled. I shoved his head back over the seat edge again. My right elbow was high, ready to smash into his throat. Do it hard enough and the man is dead.

He was making hurt noises. I looked toward the bay. The ferry was returning, maybe half a minute away.

"Going to talk?" He tried to nod his head and bleated a noise.

I let him free.

"We work for the same people," he said thickly. "You're goddamned hotheaded."

"Then don't be tricky."

The ferry bumped into the piling with a soft thud. I released my hand brake and drove down the ramp to the ferry. The man came over and collected the fare. My passenger sat there, rubbing his jaw.

No other cars came, so after another minute or two the ferry began to move across the narrow bay toward Balboa Island.

"Who are you?" I asked.

"I work for Sid Best. My name's Harry Podden."

Sid Best runs a firm of industrial and divorce detectives. If one of your employees is looting you quietly, equally quietly you get one of Sid Best's men or women to move in, get the evidence, and hustle your ex-employee off to the cops or the lonely sidewalks. Likewise if you want the stuff on your wife, or husband, Sid will furnish operators who will get the pictures, the photostats, the tape recording of the soft words of love. A rough, competent outfit.

"You're the guy who traced out Ringling Black." I was glad that I'd worked over Harry Podden a little.

"I was one of them. We didn't find much."

"Pretty clean guy."

"Too damn clean," said Podden. "You don't find them like him very often."

"Why wasn't there anything in the check-out on Black about Nile Lisbon?" I'd been wondering about that for several hours.

"This is a big deal, Oxford, you know that."

"So?"

"You're hired to get the guy into some kind of jam, aren't you?"

"You talk a hell of a lot for one of Sid Best's men."

"We both know the people who are worried about what Black can do to their candidate. You know he just lucked into that evidence, tracing down the records of one of his estate clients. He ran into a bad mess and found our candidate in the middle of it."

"I know all this. What of it?"

"The evidence is important because it's Black who has it. If he's spoiled somehow, the evidence falls apart. Nobody else would take the trouble — or the risk — of unwinding the mess again. But if Black springs it before the primaries—blooie! No more tame, well-trained candidate."

"Where do you come in now?"

"Two ways, Oxford, two ways. I'm down here on salary and expenses to watch you."

"To watch me?"

"Nobody trusts you much any more, Oxford."

I didn't say anything.

"You used to be a kind of Bill Mauldin liberal once, before all the liquor and the women and high living."

This was true, and he'd put it simply.

The ferry reached the ramp. I started the car and drove up to the street. I had intended to go to one of the night places on the Island, kick away the hours until closing time, and then, half an hour later, push open the unlocked door of the stone house on the bay. Now I had Harry Podden.

"The guys we're working for don't want you to get religion or something and maybe switch over. Just a precaution, having me watch you."

I drove toward the business area of Balboa Island, a section that looks as if it had been lifted from Beverly Hills and moved bodily to the Island.

"You're doing a lousy job of earning your salary and expenses, aren't you?"

He laughed. "I told you it's two ways. That's only one way. The other way is for me only. I want to make a little more than salary and cakes."

Of course I knew this was coming. Get in a dirty deal and you meet dirty people. We were across the street from the Park now, a standard fancy place for drinks and people who drink. I pulled into the lot and stopped.

"So how are you going to make it?"

"Through this woman, Nile Lisbon."

"Tell me more."

"You'll get a bonus of five or ten G's for framing this

joker. Probably five, but no less. Either we work this together, splitting through the middle, or I call our boys and tell them that you've already crossed them, that you've told Ringling Black that they intend to frame him. They'll believe me, and an hour later you'll be in Los Angeles city jail under enough charges to keep you in Big Q for twenty years. Do you believe me, Oxford?"

I believed him, but I didn't say anything.

"Of course, you're thinking of making your own little phone call maybe even tonight, and telling our people that Harry Podden is getting fancy ideas. Right?"

It was wrong. I was tired, disgusted, ashamed of being here, of talking about these things. Edged across the shame and disgust was a cold line of fear — Big Q, San Quentin. If the big men who had given me this job got suspicious of me, uncertain of what I'd do, they'd take quick action. A man that lives in debt, who plays around through the music-haunted, laughing night into the soft darkness of strange bedrooms, who crosses and sometimes double-crosses, is vulnerable.

All the big men would have to do would be to call a lieutenant at Hollywood station tell him carefully what the charges against Bill Oxford were. An hour or so later the black-and-white sedan with the red spotlights would stop up in Benedict Canyon or wherever I happened to be. Next the bull pen downtown, the trial, the train ride north to the terrible buildings on the bay above San Francisco. The big men had done this to other men that they suddenly mistrusted. It was all legal, deadly legal. Get in a dirty deal, meet dirty people — and then try to get out, try to get clean, buster.

We sat in the car in the half-darkness laced with the glow of neon from the shops around us.

"Before you make any call, Oxford, you'd better hear my proposition."

"Go ahead."

"The big men don't know about this Nile Lisbon woman. You and me, we know about her. It's the one soft spot in Ringling Black's whole setup."

"What's soft about it? She's the widow of his former law partner. She's got a pretty fair job. He wants to marry her. What's wrong with that?"

"You know what's wrong with it, Oxford. You fought a truck driver over that tomato today, you picked her up, and if what I hear about you is right you figure on fun and games with Nile Lisbon."

We were both quiet for a long minute.

Harry Podden talked softly now in the red-streaked darkness. "There's something wrong with Nile Lisbon. I've checked out her marriage to John Lisbon — everything O.K. Her folks live up in Riverside, she's got a brother who is a lieutenant commander in the Navy. Had a big wedding, reception at the Riverside Inn, the usual works. Marriage lasted six years, until John Lisbon's heart kicked out. Happy couple.

"After Lisbon died she went back to her folks for about six months. Then she came back to the house Lisbon had bought for her. She starts going with Black a few months later. She gets an appointment as an assistant D.A. She's a member of the bar, went to law school in L.A., where she met Lisbon, who was a visiting instructor. Just one other item: She likes truck drivers, bartenders, musicians, lifeguards, fishermen — and she goes off for very quiet week ends with them.

"She does this so smooth that nobody in this damn gossiping, nosy county even suspects that Nile Lisbon ever plays around."

"Do you see the frame we can fix now, Oxford? Maybe you don't know it, but Ringling Black is crazy in love with this tomato, and he doesn't know what she is!"

"What's the frame, Podden?"

"The old stuff. We get this Lisbon babe caught cold — pictures and the rest. Then it's up to Black. He turns the evidence on the candidate over to us, or Nile Lisbon gets shown up in Orange County for the bum she is."

"How do you fit in, Podden?"

"I want half of the dough you get. I've earned it, I've done the work and I need the dough. If you go along with me, Oxford, we can be counting the hundred-dollar bills by next week. I've got my camera. I've got infrared film for some nice work in the dark, and I've got a tape recorder. I know how to do the job. I've done it a hundred times for divorce deals. How about it, Oxford?"

"Why didn't they hire you in the first place?"

His voice got a whining edge. "They had to have a big shot, a Bill Oxford, not just a punk with sore feet like Harry Podden."

Well, that was it. Podden smelled money like a shark smelling blood. He wouldn't leave until his sharp teeth had torn into the life of Nile Lisbon and he'd had her golden blood.

"Where you staying, Podden?"

"That doesn't matter. Are you in with me?"

"If I'm not?"

"I need the dough, Oxford. I could use all of it."

"Get moving, Podden."

"That your answer Oxford?"

"Mr. Oxford to you — and if you ever forget that, I'll beat you soft. Get out!"

He started to talk and I hit him hard, my fist catching the corner of his mouth and his cheek. He swung open the door and scrambled out.

"I'll see you, Mr. Oxford."

I watched him run a few steps, turn, and look back. Then he walked away, a lonely, dangerous little shark with poison teeth, swimming in the dark waters of the night.

This was not a time for me to be alone, thinking. None of the thoughts would be much good. I went into the Park and started drinking, fast, like a man who wants to lose himself.

By the time it was two and the places were closing it was pretty hard to get to my car. I was staggering a lot now. Instead of taking the ferry, I drove over the causeway to the mainland and U.S. 101. I circled back around the bay, coming back into the long, low sand peninsula of Newport and Balboa.

I was drunk enough to have trouble finding the house on the bay. When I found it, I parked a block away, with the shrewdness of the drunk, and lurched toward the house, holding to the high walls in front of the other houses as I staggered.

The front door of the stone house was unlocked. I pushed it open, locked it behind me, and tried to climb the lighted stairs. I was very drunk.

I looked up. She was standing at the top of the stairs, looking down at the lurching, falling man below her.

CHAPTER SIX

Nile Lisbon still wore the simple green-striped dress she had worn that afternoon. I tried to focus my eyes, said something thickly.

"You got drunk, Bill Oxford. Why?" She stepped down a little way, held out a small hand toward me.

I reached for her hand, missed it, grabbed it, almost pulled her downstairs toward me.

"Come on, boy, you'll make it. Easy and steady," she said. She was smiling a little. Somehow I got to the top of the stairs. The living room of the house was on this floor, with a long series of big ceiling-to-floor windows opening on a balcony over the bay. I sat down like a fighter hitting his stool after a tough round.

Nile stood in front of me, one hand on my shoulder, and the smile was gone. She looked, now, as a woman does when she needs to ask for something, something of desperate, final importance; needs to ask and is afraid of the answer. But she said nothing.

"Door was open, like you said," I mumbled, and I suppose I tried to grin at her. I was sliding down, away, and for a moment I had the drunk's spotlight of clarity — the brief time of realizing that I was stupid, helpless drunk. I tried to get up, shook my head, and rolled sideways, hiding my eyes with the rough cloth of my sleeve.

"Bill. Bill ..." I could hear her voice, felt her fingers on my face. My eyes were too heavy to open, my tongue was too thick to talk.

"Why did you need to be drunk, Bill?" Her voice was a clear whisper, close to my ear. I was stretched out on something, a couch, my left arm over my eyes, my right arm dangling. I could hear her and that was about all I knew.

"I'm not like that, Bill. Whatever you think, however it looks, I'm not like that." The clear whisper was for herself; she didn't know that I hadn't slipped out completely. Nile was speaking to Nile, as if she were writing a letter to me in whispers, but a letter that only she would ever read.

"There has to be a man, Bill. A woman has to have a man. Until she has one she's in hell.

"But some of them are strong — and nothing else. Some of them are smart and weak. A few — a few are strong, and they have something more, but they don't know what love is. They'll take a woman the way they'd take a bottle of whisky.

"I had a good man. God, aren't there any more good men? Not one?"

Her voice had an empty loneliness.

It was dark when I opened my eyes again. My coat, shirt, and shoes were off, and I was on the couch, covered with a soft blanket. I sat up, remembered where I was. My mouth was filled with something like dry, dirty cotton. A drink would fix that — there had to be a drink around somewhere. I pushed back the blanket, stood up. Still drunk, but not with the stumbling, lurching drunkenness of before. It was five in the morning.

Find Nile, get a drink. Find Nile, make love to her. I rubbed my face and walked toward the row of windows. Maybe some air would do me good. The big room was dark, and the night beyond the windows was solid black. I looked backward. There was a dim light on the stairs. The almost full moon that had ridden the skies above the thin fog was gone.

Somewhere in the house there'd be a bedroom and Nile would be there. I went back through the dark room, and I fell across a low table.

As I pushed the overturned table away from me and got up, I saw her in the doorway. She was small, the curve of her cheek lit by the lamp on the stairway, a small, dark figure, shadowy.

"Nile."

"Are you hurt, Bill?"

I went to her, quietly, and put my arms around her, hunted her mouth with mine. She pushed at me with her hands, tried to say something, and then I found her.

It was stepping out of reality into something I had never known before. This was the whirlpool.

Sometimes I would try to say something, a fragment of a word, a quick whisper of "Nile!" Nothing else. The drunkenness burned away, and I forgot everything but Nile.

There was no exhaustion, no satiety. In time, a long time, there was a gray light on the long row of windows, a rim of light over the roundness of the hills.

Then we talked. Sometimes now her eyes were warm and she smiled, and sometimes there was only that look of waiting desperation, the eyes wide, lips apart. But our talk was good, and she made coffee for us as we sat in the big room with day coming over the hills beyond the bay.

It was good talk, but we weren't honest. Neither of us.

"You're the only woman that's ever been important to me." This was true.

"Why? I'm not much. Bill. I need so much and I have

so little to give in return."

"I don't know, Nile. I know what I said is true."

I didn't ask her any questions in the dawn hour. I never would ask Nile Lisbon any questions. I thought, and then within minutes I asked her an unfair one.

She asked only one and it was a tough question.

"Why are you here in Newport, Bill? Job? Vacation?"

"A very dirty job."

She looked at me patiently as if to say that she didn't believe me, or that I was joking. Maybe her patience meant that she didn't care how dirty the job was.

"I'm down here to frame Ringling Black." Be a complete fool, Oxford, and the grand championship in being a fool always goes to the man who tells a woman.

"I don't understand, Bill."

"I've been offered five thousand dollars to get Black into a jam so bad that he'll either turn over the stuff he's got on a certain candidate or — "

"You mean the stuff he found when he was handling the Soames estate?"

"I guess that was it. The stuff that shows the candidate to have embezzled a lot of money, taken bribes from other crooks, and got mixed up in a very slimy situation with a sixteen-year-old. Black's got it all; we can't let it out."

"Who is we, Bill?"

"The people who offered me the five thousand. The people behind the candidate."

The windows over the bay showed a luminous gray now, the early sun through the morning fog.

"Why are you in a deal like this, Bill?" Her hand went out to mine, warm and firm.

"I need the money. What else?"

"Ringling Black is a good, decent man."

I was like a hurt animal, hiding my hurt, ready to lash out. "If he's so damn good and decent, why don't you marry him?"

"I wouldn't be good for him, and he isn't what I need." Her hand was still on mine. It was a fair answer to an unfair question.

"So I'm down here on a dirty deal. Now what do you think of your Bill Oxford?"

She kissed me and it was the whirlpool and the hunger, the only answer she knew.

At seven she made breakfast. We hadn't talked about Ringling Black again. We talked now of things we could do together. A yawl in the wind off Dana Point. Horses on the Sierra trails. Swordfish, and the royal swordfish, the marlin, in the bright summer seas near Catalina. Sun and sand at Ensenada, watching the long translucent rollers break into foam. We sounded as if we meant to do all these things together.

"Now I have to dress into my assistant D.A. outfit and go off to Santa Ana," she said as she rinsed off the breakfast dishes.

"Aren't you going to be a little bit tired?"

"Tired? I feel wonderful." She looked wonderful.

Her arms were around me. "Whatever you do, whoever you have to hurt — that's your business, Bill. I don't care if you're the worst guy in the world, or if you do terrible things to good people. If you are true to yourself I'll be with you, no matter what you do or who you do it to. Do you understand, darling?"

"If I'm true to myself?"

"If you do these things because you want to, and not because you're weak or afraid. You don't have to be good, but you have to be strong, be strong and smart and know what love means. I need that in a man, darling. I don't need anything else."

There with her, at that moment, I felt plenty strong, plenty smart, and I knew what love meant. The doubts didn't come, any of them, while I stood there in the little kitchen with her.

She dressed. Her "assistant D.A. outfit" was another simple belted dress, this time something extra in cotton with a pattern somehow like the colors of a summer evening, dark blues, but still a background of brightness.

"Want me to drive you, darling?" she asked.

"My car's a block away. I'll take my time and then go over to the Inn. I've got a room there."

"The Inn's nice."

"This is nicer. How about neighbors?"

"The other two houses are empty until summer, except for kids during Easter week." She went to the stairs and I walked down with her.

At the door I said, "When?"

She looked surprised. "Tonight, of course."

"Where?"

"Anywhere. Sometimes I can leave as early as two or three."

"Christian's. I'll be there from three on."

"Don't get too drunk, my darling."

"I'll never want to get drunk again, Nile."

When she had left the good feeling lasted a little while and then the small gray mice in my mind nibbled it away. I didn't feel so strong and so smart now.

Somewhere in this little town of Newport and Balboa was Harry Podden. The only way I could handle Podden was the way I had handled others like him in these past few years. Beat him up, put the fear into him. And then I had to get to work on Ringling Black.

If the big men in the fine offices back in Los Angeles got annoyed with me I wouldn't see Nile Lisbon except on visiting day at Big Q. Last night I had known, but I hadn't looked carefully. This morning the gray mice in my mind nibbled away at the things I'd tried to hide. A few hundred dollars in checks that one of the big men was holding, all mine, none of them any good. A couple of deals that I'd worked on in the last year in which I'd sworn to false statements to clear a kid I knew who was in a rough go. He was clear, all right — he'd been killed on a curve going to Arrowhead last Thanksgiving Day — but the false statements signed under each oath by Bill Oxford were in somebody's safe in Los Angeles.

If they wanted to get me, they had me, cold.

I made myself another cup of coffee, found a bottle of brandy in the kitchen, and had that best of morning drinks.

The one thing I didn't want to think about for a while was Nile Lisbon, but the small mice wouldn't leave that part of my mind alone either. This was everything that the dark eyes had promised when I first saw them. This was everything — but how much of it was honest? Was there any honesty in Nile Lisbon?

Probably not. She'd fooled two men that I knew about yesterday. King McCarthy and Ringling Black, she had fooled them as if she spent every day of her life picking up men in bars by looking over the shoulder of the lad she was with, as if she was used to saying goodnight to one man and leaving her door open for another.

The mice had a fine chance to scamper around behind my eyes when I went to the closet to find my coat. At the far end of the closet was a leather jacket. It not only looked like part of King's uniform; it had "T/Sgt King McCarthy" and a serial number stenciled across the back of it.

Usually men like King don't lie to other men, but King had. The poor son-of-a-bitch was probably in love with Nile Lisbon too.

CHAPTER SEVEN

Downstairs, out of the door, locking it, and into the gray coolness of an early-spring Friday morning. Nothing ahead of me but trouble, nothing behind me but regrets. It's a hell of a way to begin a day in spring.

My car had been parked badly, one front wheel over the curb. I slid in behind the wheel. She was a tramp, I'd known she was a tramp yesterday. I turned the key, pushed the starter. The Merc was pretty warmhearted, and I felt the easy whir of power. I wheeled back from the curb, feeling the small bump as the misused tire rolled off the edge. I swung around the bay-front street and headed for the Inn.

Nothing about Oxford that's so damn charming, not any more there isn't. Six even, one-eighty, beach-club tan, still fairly solid across the arms, and shoulders, a place where there should be a soft belly but the soft belly had been kept hard and flat by big Swedes at the club, by all the things a guy can do that are fun, like swimming, riding, golf. Not by work. But there's something about the eyes and mouth that's not good.

Oxford doesn't have anything for Nile Lisbon — but

then, she doesn't have anything for him either. I jammed the wheel to round a corner too fast and squealing. Who was I lying to — me? I was anxious and hungry to see her again, eager.

So she's a tramp. What the hell am I? She isn't as pretty, not as smooth, not as skillful as any of twenty girls in the last couple of years — but I can't remember their faces, not even their names, now. And that's the way it is, because this one woman is as real to me now, here driving the few blocks to the Inn, as if we were back in the room with the wide windows and the dawn rimming the edge of the hills. Why? What man ever knows why?

I needed a drink and it was still too early for any of the fancy bars on the Balboa end of the peninsula to be open. The fishermen's bars in Newport would be open, they'd be open at six in the morning.

Some of the kids were arriving for their nine days already. As I drove north along the street toward the Newport end, the MG's and the top-down convertibles were on the other side headed for the rented homes and the motels along the bay. Kids with nothing but fun and excitement ahead of them, nothing much but childhood behind them. A wonderful way to start a morning in spring.

Tug's was open and busy. The red-faced man was behind the bar listening to a fisherman talking about the boat he was going to buy.

"Bourbon, straight. Soda on the side." The barman looked at me, recognizing me, remembering me. He probably had me tagged — a joker who gets in trouble over women.

He poured it, I paid for it, I drank it. It went down like a red hot lizard. Not the whisky's fault, but maybe the time, or maybe the drinker.

"How you doin'?" asked the barman.

"Great. How else?"

He looked skeptical, moved along, and polished some glasses. The fisherman was ready to talk some more about the boat he was going to buy. A couple of men at the end of the bar were talking about who lost the most in the poker game they had been in last night. I remembered the hundred I'd gone for — without reason, just to be doing something that cost money.

It was time to face up to the trouble ahead today. Podden and Black.

It was still too early to call any of the big men up in Los Angeles. I walked out of Tug's, got in my car, and drove to the motel where I had left Ann Field last night. I parked on the street beyond the banana trees in front of the place and walked to the cottage I remembered. I tried the door. It was unlocked, so I knocked.

"Who is it?" Her voice sounded all right.

"Bill Oxford."

"Oh. Come in."

She didn't look bad, one of those girls who look a dozen times better sober than they do drunk. Any woman does, come to think of it.

Same clothes as last night, of course. A little too dressy — a skirt of soft material that looks like silver wool, an embroidered jacket, something under the jacket that was sheer and gold in color. But still some of the girl who had once been so young and fresh and lovely was there this morning.

"Thanks for getting me out of the rain last night, Bill." The vicious hatred of last night was gone now, too, or hidden.

"Lots of alcohol."

"Too much, Bill. But you know how it is sometimes. I had to come down to Balboa, somehow, this year. The place has memories for me. Good memories, mostly."

"I know, Ann."

"A woman gets like that. Things are no good, so she goes to the place where they used to be good."

I didn't say anything.

"Sit down, Bill. Have breakfast yet?"

"Not yet," I lied.

"Care to have company?"

She was so much like the Ann I knew six years or so back.

"Sure."

"Remember the place in the pavilion, on the bay front, with all the glass so you can see the boats? Remember when the whole crowd of us had breakfast there every morning during Easter week?"

"We'll go there, Ann."

"I've got an overnight bag at the bus station, but I'll pick it up after breakfast. What are you down here for, Bill? I hate to say it, but we're both about five years too old for Easter week."

She smiled, a nice girl smile. All of the bitterness, the viciousness of the drunken woman last night were gone from the girl of this morning. It didn't make me feel good, it made me feel sick and dirty.

"Ready, Bill?" She swirled around in front of the wall mirror.

"Ready, Ann."

We went out to my car, drove the short distance to the casino or pavilion, an old, ornate wooden building. The cafe was on the first floor, in a corner toward the bay. A waitress in a crisp light-blue uniform took our orders for orange juice, bacon, and eggs. We had coffee first.

Ann talked about kids we had known — they'd been kids, five, six, seven years ago. One guy had gone back to the Air Force, two of the girls had families now, two more of them were married to guys who had been in our crowd. Stuff like that, but it was all news from a couple of years back. Ann had not heard anything lately, but neither of us mentioned that.

"The folks sold the orange grove and moved to Los Angeles," Ann told me, "and they like it fine. They've a sweet little place, almost downtown. They don't do anything, just go to the park or whatever they want. You know what they do mostly, Bill? Go to radio and television shows. Imagine Mom doing that!"

After breakfast I drove her to the bus depot, back in Newport, and she picked up her overnight case. A nice one of alligator, badly scuffed.

"I didn't bring much, Bill. I wasn't sure how long I'd stay. Then there's my job, too."

"Your job?"

For the first time this morning her lips thinned, the corners down, and then she smiled. "Modeling. High-fashion stuff, mostly. But I think I'll get an office job. Just nine to five every day. It'll be a change. But I'm doing wonderfully."

We were in my car, outside the tired-looking bus station.

"I thought you said things were no good."

She was too quick in her answer. "I meant I was tired of the city, and my job and everything. All I want to do is stretch out on the sand and watch the sky and the kids. Like we used to do. Remember, Bill?"

"I've got a job for you," I said evenly, with the bitterness searing across my guts, and my heart, if I had any left. "You can pick up a quick couple of hundred."

"Oh."

I knew she would say, "Oh," like that. It was the sound a hope might have made before it died, a small hope that had just been beaten to death. It took seconds to die, that small hope, because she was quiet for long, terrible seconds.

"What's the job? Who is the man and what makes me worth a couple of bills?" Flat, dead voice from a tired old face.

"Some big people want a guy framed. No matter what you or I do, this guy is going to get it anyway. But if we do it — "

"You get paid. I get paid. O.K." Contempt can be like the thin edge of a razor, so fine that all you know of its touch is the blood that begins to ooze.

"It has to be quick and rough. Today, maybe."

"What do I do?"

"He's a lawyer. See him at his office. Get him to meet you with his car. Just before you get in the car, you drink some chloral hydrate. On the way there tear your clothes, scream, get out of the car screaming. Tell the cops that he gave you a drink in the car and that it tasted funny, then you began to get woozy and he tried to attack you. Make sure they pump out your stomach."

"All that for two lousy bills?"

"How many girls do you know would do it for one?"

"I told you, you lousy crumb, last night. I'll kill you someday. I've got to be drunk to do it, but I'll do it. O.K., I'll do your dirt for you."

"It'll have to be today. Things are ganging up on me. You phone this man's office this morning — make an appointment for this afternoon. Build it up all you need so that he'll drive you to Laguna to see a man you're buying some property from. Got that clear?"

"What's the guy's name?"

"Ringling Black. His office is in Balboa. Black and Packard."

"I've heard of him. When we lived near here — wasn't it Lisbon and Black, something like that?" She was a businesswoman now; the small hope was gone.

"Lisbon's been dead a couple of years. It's Black that we've got to get short — and today."

"How much now?"

I looked at her and shook my head. We knew each other, knew each other the way we were now, not as we once had been. "Two bills when Black's in jail with you preferring charges against him."

"I'm nearly flat. I came here with twenty and I drank a lot of that up last night."

I gave her another twenty.

"No drinking until just before you go up to his office. Time it fast. The chloral starts working in about ten minutes. That will give you time to see him, get in his car, and get on the highway. When you feel it begin to hit, ask him to drive off the road, swing the door open, tear your clothes, and start screaming on the highway. There's plenty of traffic. By that time you'll be out.

"Your story — after they pump your guts out — is that you met Black in Los Angeles weeks ago and he invited you down here for an afternoon with friends of his. How clean are you?"

"You mean have I ever been picked up by the cops? Never. Not yet."

"Go back to the motel where I registered you last night. You've got your place there until noon, anyway. Be real sweet, and friendly. Tell them you came down for an afternoon with Ringling Black. Talk about people you used to know around here. Got it?"

"Yeah."

"When you call his office, probably an office girl will answer. Tell her that it's Miss Ann Field for Mr. Black. If she asks what it's about, say it's personal. Oh, yes — tell the motel people that you came down on the bus yesterday but that an old friend, Bill Oxford, registered you in last night. You and I had better have lunch today at Christian's Hut. About one."

"The slick Bill Oxford is willing to involve himself?"

"I'm clean on the deal. I can back you up when the cops check you."

"Sweet of you, you lousy crumb."

"Forget that stuff. You've got to act like you did at breakfast."

She didn't say anything. I drove her to the motel.

"What do I tell the mark?"

"Black?"

"That's what I said, the mark. What do I tell him?"

"Ask what time he'll be free to drive you to Laguna and give you some advice on transfer of property. Make sure that you're talking to him on a closed line."

"O.K."

"Where have you been living in L.A., Ann?"

She gave me a twisted smile. "I've got an address with a couple of girls."

"Are they clean?"

She shrugged her shoulders. "Not very. But they've never been arrested either."

"Write it out for me." I gave her a card and she

scribbled an address and phone number.

"See you at one at the Hut." I carried her bag to the motel office and went back to my car. This time I drove to the Inn. While I was there I changed clothes and shaved.

Chloral hydrate is not easy to get and the possession of it is a felony. But I had an ounce of the stuff in my suitcase. I'd had it for several weeks.

Go back to last Christmas. Big party at a place in Brentwood, a mixed-up crowd of important names, chiselers, crashers, and people like me. I spotted a man and woman that I'd scared away from a blackmail trap they had set up for a guy at CBS. I saw them before they saw me. The party was plenty large, with lots of action, and after a time I got the guy alone in a corridor. We had a little trouble and after he was talking again he told me his story.

They had a mark set up. A top writer for television who had a nice wife he loved. The wife was at Palm Springs with their children and the writer was driving there for Christmas morning. The deal the man and the woman had in mind was for him to give them a ride to the Springs after the party. On the way the writer would get a drink laced with chloral. He'd wake up in a motel the next morning with the woman and plenty of witnesses around. They figured a twenty-thousand take.

In the course of telling me all this and wiping the blood off his face, the man gave me the ounce of chloral hydrate. Maybe he had figured on a frame for me somehow, and then realized that I'd left his fingerprints on the vial. I kept the stuff. The people at the party knew that Oxford and some guy had a beef, and that's all any of them — including the writer —

ever knew. That Oxford — troublemaker and kind of shady. It goes like that.

I'd put the vial in my suitcase and now I put it in my pocket. If I got picked up and searched, for any reason, by the local law, my possession of the stuff was a one-year ticket, at least. Maybe Nile Lisbon would have the interesting job of prosecuting me.

Funny.

I went downstairs and walked along the ocean, in the rolling dunes.

It was almost an hour before I got straight. I'd walked to Newport and back, not looking at the sand, the sky, or the sea — looking into Bill Oxford.

Then it happened and I said to hell with them. It came, in the end, that fast.

Out towards the rim of the ocean I could see the small boats of the fishermen. Thick-fingered guys with sturdy backs and clear eyes. What would they think of something like Bill Oxford?

I'd been a proud guy once.

For months now, maybe for years, this had been building up in me. I'd learned to despise the people I was with, the girls with masks for faces and lizard eyes, the soft scheming men, lying with a smile when they needed you, cruel and arrogant when they didn't.

Watching the fishermen on the gray sea, I thought of the people I knew now. I despised them — tortured, squirming animals in good clothes, nibbling at fine food, knotted and bound by things that didn't matter. Which table they were led to at Romanoff's, whether to buy a Mark VII or a Sunbeam Alpine, how they were mentioned in the *Reporter*, whose women they'd sleep with at Vegas on the next week end. For things like that they rotted away their lives. I despised them, and yet they were all that I knew now. And they despised me.

Rightly so. If they crept with soft mouths and wet tongues for the hands of the important, and if they snarled at those less important, I did so too.

I felt sick. Men in battle turn sick in their guts when they realize their own cowardice, as if their bodies were trying to express their self-hate. I hated Bill Oxford.

A man can hate himself only to a point; then he has to do something.

I took the vial out, pulled the stopper, let the stuff pour into the sand, and scuffed it over.

No five thousand. To hell with the five thousand and the stuff money had been buying me.

The big men would be angry. To hell with the big men. Their anger was a lot more decent than their satisfaction with me.

San Quentin. To hell with San Quentin. If that was what I had to take to be able to look at myself in a mirror, I'd take it, and three years there would maybe be better than the last three. Better than seeing yourself rot like a piece of meat in the sun, with only flies for friends.

I threw the empty vial far out into the surf.

There was no percentage in hating yourself, no percentage in seeing your pride in yourself as a man die. No percentage in any of that — and they all said that Bill Oxford was a percentage player.

The morning fog was thin now, and the sun was an orange high above the hills beyond Balboa and the bay.

Once you face up to it, the whole damn world is different. You feel strong and smart again, as you did on *Yank*, as you did with Nile Lisbon this morning.

She had said it. "I don't care if you're the worst guy in the world, if you are true to yourself." She had said, "Not because you're weak or afraid. You have to be strong, and smart, and know what love means."

Nile had it right. Whatever was true of me, now, was true of Nile. I was in love with Nile; we could try to work out the rest. If we couldn't work it out, at least we would have tried with the best that was in us. That's pretty good love. I felt good, thoroughly good for the first time in a long while.

The bar at the Inn was open but I didn't need a drink; I needed a telephone. I called the courthouse in Santa Ana. Santa Ana is the big town of the county, around fifty thousand, inland about fourteen miles. First there was the courthouse switchboard, then somebody in the D.A.'s office, and then the soft, clear voice of Nile Lisbon.

"Hello?"

"This is Bill Oxford, darling. I love you."

"Bill."

"The Hut. At three?"

"At three, darling."

"Good-by, Nile." I hung up. A lot of words weren't necessary.

The slot took several quarters for the Los Angeles call. He was in and willing to talk to me, the big man behind the candidate, the big man who had hired me for the Ringling Black job.

He talked first. "That was damn fast work, Oxford. When I want something fixed, you'll do my fixing. Good job, kid."

"I've got to tell you — "

He overrode my voice. "I know all about it, Oxford.

You moved right in and got him where it hurts. Finish it up, bring in Black's endorsement of our candidate, and your five thousand is ready for you."

"What are you talking about?"

"The pictures. Podden called me about ten minutes ago and said that all the infrared shots of you and the Lisbon woman came out clear and sharp. He told me what those pictures would do to the Lisbon woman, and how much Black thought of her. Nice work."

The balcony behind the wide windows, before dawn. I wondered how long Podden had waited in the darkness, how close I had been to him when I stood by the window.

"Get Black's letter right up here and pick up the money, Oxford, I'm throwing a party tonight and you're welcome, fellow. You might even get some girls, hey?"

CHAPTER EIGHT

The tough thing is when you get it right between the eyes and you know in your heart you deserve it. Smart Bill Oxford had taken it, and I knew that I had it coming.

Out in the gray-streaked sunlight, with the surf booming along the shore, I walked slowly, alone under a sky that was too big, before an ocean that was too big. A little while ago I had told Nile Lisbon that I loved her. Harry Podden could prove with pictures that we loved each other — or at least had gone through the motions of love.

Action would be the answer now. I walked back along the ocean front, turned at the street in Balboa that led to Ringling Black's office.

He was in, the girl at the desk told me. She wanted to know my name and my business, pleasant enough about it.

"Oxford. The business is personal." I stood in front of her desk, looking down at her, a small girl in a neat suit.

"Does Mr. Black know you, Mr. Oxford?"

"We met last night."

"I see." She went to a door at the side of the small anteroom, knocked, then opened it and stepped inside. When she came back she looked at me with a new interest, an open curiosity, as if she had just learned something strange about me.

"He'll see you. Through that door, please." She remained standing, her head turning slowly as I walked by her.

Black was standing too, at the side of his desk, and he looked at me with the same kind of curiosity his secretary had shown. He did not hold out his hand to me and he was not smiling.

"Whatever you'd planned to say, Oxford, don't say it." His voice had the coldness of contempt, not the heat of anger. "You can get out of this town right now on your own power. If you don't, I'll throw you out. Understand?"

"You know why I'm here?" We were standing three feet apart, facing each other. Ringling Black was a big man; he looked like a strong man.

"Yes."

"Harry Podden has been here already?"

I could see that Black did not recognize the name. "Who?"

"A private detective. Harry Podden."

"Is he in this blackmail frame with you?"

So Ringling Black had the big answer already — but he didn't know Podden. Both of us, standing there, staring into each other's eyes, were puzzled.

"Yes."

"You can take him with you. When you leave this office, Oxford, start moving. Go back to Los Angeles and tell your crowd that they can try any dirty trick they want. The evidence on their filthy, slimy crook of a candidate will be shown to every voter in California tonight. Five minutes ago I made arrangements for fifteen minutes of television time tonight. When I'm done, the people of this state might vote to lynch your candidate — but that's the only way they'd vote for him. Now get out!"

I stood there. The candidate might mean fifty million in contracts for the big men back in Los Angeles, the evidence against him might mean the dignity of civic decency to Ringling Black, but this mess meant only Nile Lisbon to me. To Bill Oxford the important thing was a small woman with shining hair and deep dark eyes.

"How much do you know?" I asked.

"A girl came here a little while ago. Miss Field, Miss Ann Field. She told me what you were bribing her to do. I can guess who's behind you. That's all I need to know."

Ann Field, beaten, corrupted, debased, had played it straight. I felt a cool gladness because of Ann.

"That's all you know?"

His eyes never left mine. "That's enough, Oxford."

"There's more, Black. I have to get the rest of it straight with you, too."

I had known what I was risking when I had come here. It was a double risk, a curious one. What I intended to do might mean San Quentin for me — the ruthless anger of the most powerful men in California. I was throwing away everything I had, everything except my self-respect. I was hoping to find that again, when everything else was gone.

The other risk concerned this man. Somehow, desperately, I hoped that he would play it straight too. I hoped that he would sacrifice Nile rather than give in. Maybe I wanted an atonement, a punishment for both of us, and I wanted that punishment to buy something good, a million votes' worth of decency and honesty.

"You have to get the rest of what straight, Oxford?"

There were two quick raps on the door behind us. The neat little secretary opened the door and bent her head forward. "A man who says his business is very urgent — an emergency, Mr. Black. His name is Mr. Podden, Harry Podden."

Black's eyebrows went up. "Podden?" He looked at me. "Send him in now, please."

Harry edged into the room, saw me, stopped. He was timid, frightened, but bold and greedy too. He looked at me nervously, as if he were trying to guess how much physical danger this room held for him.

"Don't pay any attention to this man, Mr. Black," Podden blurted, his small face still marked from my fists. "He's out of the deal. I'm the man you have to talk to now."

I reached out and grabbed Podden by the throat of his shirt, pulled him toward me. The secretary screamed in a small, neat voice, a little scream. Black grabbed my arms, locked them. He was strong.

Podden tore loose and hit me in the face. I tried to break away from Black.

"I'll have both of you thrown in jail," said Black. "Stand apart. Right now!" The lawyer had other kinds of strength besides muscle; his voice had authority. Podden backed away from me, his hands still up. Black eased his hold on my arms and I let them fall to my sides.

"I've got the pictures, Mr. Black. This fellow didn't work this out — I did. I'll make the deal with you, not him." Podden almost squeaked in his nervous urgency. This was possibly the biggest thing the little man had ever dared and he was trembling now.

"What pictures?" Black narrowed his eyes, his chin jutted forward. This was something new and he was waiting for it like an animal, a shrewd, powerful animal that hears the sound of a deadly enemy. Black knew the power of the big men.

"The pictures of this fellow and the Lisbon woman. You can have them — negatives and all the prints — if you make a deal with me."

Black's eyes were narrowed to cold, bright lines. His face showed no emotion.

"When were these pictures taken?"

"Last night, early this morning. At her home. Infrared in the darkness. Good, clear pictures." Podden had begun by chattering, but toward the end his voice was slower, as if he knew that once again he had missed — somehow not smart enough, somehow not strong enough, the way it had been all his life.

The door clicked closed. The neat secretary had stepped out quietly, discreetly.

Black looked at me, his eyelids lifting slowly until they were fully open. It was an odd look, first appraising and questioning as if to measure me in a new light, and then there was something that I felt was pity. He lifted his phone, told his secretary to get Mrs. Lisbon at the Santa Ana courthouse. The three of us were silent, waiting for the call to be complete.

"Hello, Nile? My dear ..." Black hesitated. This was not easy for him. He waited for a moment and began again. "There are two blackmailers in my office. One of them is a private detective named Podden, the other is this fellow Oxford. They're trying to make a deal with me ... Yes, blackmailers." He listened for long seconds and spoke again. "They say they have pictures of you taken last night, you and Oxford. I haven't seen them, I don't want to see them. Could it be true Nile?"

I could see his fingers whiten with pressure on the phone's smooth black plastic.

"I understand," he said slowly.

My hands shot out and I took the phone away from him. "Nile! Nile!" I shouted into the dead plastic and metal. There was only the humming of a disconnected line. I stood there holding the thing and looking at it.

"Let's make our deal, Mr. Black," said Harry Podden.

"There won't be any deal," said Ringling Black.

"Damn right there won't be any!" I dropped the humming phone and my hands closed around Podden's throat before he could get away from me. Podden kicked viciously and he tried with his left thumb for my eye. Black hit me solidly behind the ear and I went to my knees. Podden kicked me again, turned, and swung open the door. Black hit me on the side of my face and I went to the floor, rolling on my side. Black stood above me, waiting.

I pushed myself up. My hands went down. I didn't want to fight Black, and Podden was gone.

"Now, before I beat you into a piece of rotten meat, get out!"

If I could have talked to him, explained that he was right about everything except what I was now and why I had come to him, but there was no chance. You can see when a man is ready to fight to the death, and Ringling Black was ready. I walked unsteadily toward the door. Maybe I could whip him, but he wanted to kill me and I had no anger against him. It would not be a good fight and there would be nothing gained by it. The neat little secretary backed against the wall as I went by her.

When I reached the outer door Black was behind me. "Whenever I see you, wherever I see you, I'll smash you into the nearest gutter, you cheap, slimy blackmailer!"

I rubbed my face when I reached the street. Black could hit hard and solid. The sun rode high in the blue-gray sky and the street was already loud with the Easter-week crowd, girls in swimsuits, boys in bright trunks. Convertibles, MG's and a borrowed family sedan or two were strung along the curb, bumper tight.

The whipped dog that was Bill Oxford slunk along the street. Maybe it was the kids more than anything else that made me realize what I was. The laughing kids with all the world in front of them, and nine days of excitement and the best of love ready for them now. By evening there would be thousands of them in Balboa.

Count it off on your fingers, chump, I thought. Count the things you've lost. The old, cheap, lousy, comfortable phony-big-shot life of the last few years — that's gone. You were willing to trade it in, and pay a good price along with the trade, on a little self-respect, and the strange, wild love that Nile Lisbon means to you.

Count that one off too. Nile Lisbon has just been told that you tried to blackmail Ringling Black with pictures of the two of you last night. Count off the strange, deep, satisfying excitement that is love with Nile Lisbon.

Count everything off on your fingers, chump, you've had it. Nothing left.

One thing. A little happiness in a girl named Ann Field. For whatever her reasons, at least she played it straight. She left you and went to Ringling Black to tell him that Bill Oxford was setting up a blackmail plot against him and that she wouldn't go through with it.

Ann Field knew what that might mean — playing it straight and crossing Bill Oxford, the fixer for the big men, cold, ruthless, powerful. It might have meant a couple of years in a women's penitentiary on a quick frame, or a working over by a couple of the hard boys that would leave her face an ugly toothless ruin. She was risking a lot and she had known it when she went to Ringling Black.

At least I was glad for her. And that was the only thing in all the world the smart, smooth operator Bill Oxford had to be glad about.

I went into the phone booth of the Balboa Inn and called the Santa Ana courthouse. Mrs. Lisbon had left her office and she would not be back until Monday, so a cool secretarial voice told me.

Do something, Oxford. Don't stand here under the fog-veiled sun and listen to the laughter of the kids who are beginning their nine days of Easter in the never-never town of Balboa between the bay and the sea.

I did something. I found Harry Podden's home address in the phone books of the hotel. Not in Los Angeles Central, or the Western, or the Southeastern, but in the Long Beach directory. Long Beach, really a part of the spreading swarm of Los Angeles, was only a few minutes' drive from Newport-Balboa. Podden lived on Lindon Avenue in Long Beach.

Twenty minutes later I cruised on Linden, looking at the numbers on the small, tired stucco houses. Podden's house was stucco, gray and yellow now rather than the white it had been thirty years ago. Someone had tried to keep a little garden of flowers in front and had grown tired of trying. There were two children in front, a spindly boy of nine or ten, a snuffling little girl of three or four. The boy was bouncing a ball, and the girl was playing among the husks of dead flowers.

I stopped my car along the curb and got out. "You kids know a Mr. Podden?"

The boy stopped bouncing his ball. "Sure, he's our dad."

"Is he home?"

"No. He's out catching bad people. That's what my dad does. He's a detective and he catches bad people. Sometimes they try to shoot him, but my dad's real brave. He isn't scared of bullets or anything. He's a real detective. Some of the kids around here won't believe my dad's a real detective, but he is, he's brave and he catches all the bad people."

The spindly little boy said all this breathlessly, his eyes big and round in his thin pale face.

"Do you think he's coming home soon?"

"Soon as he catches all the bad people for today. That's going to take a long time, because he called Mamma a little while ago and said he wouldn't be home until real late. How late is real late, mister? Is twelve o'clock real late?"

"It sure is, son. Thanks a lot."

I began to pull out from the curb.

"You believe my dad's a real detective, don't you, mister?"

"Yes, son. I believe it."

"Good-by, mister. Wave at the man, Sandra. Wave bye at the man."

The little girl kept playing in the dirt around the flower husks, snuffling a little.

Whatever I did, whatever I would have to do, at least I wouldn't do it on Linden Avenue in Long Beach. I drove back to Newport and Balboa.

CHAPTER NINE

I recognized Nile's car in the thickening stream of traffic along Central in Newport. It was a car ahead of me and I tried to pass but the road was too narrow, too jammed with cars full of young men and girls. The thousands were pouring into the narrow sand pit of the peninsula, heading towards the motels and rented homes of Balboa.

She stayed a car ahead of me until we reached Balboa and then I swung around a '53 Chev convertible, gunned the Mercury, and moved alongside of Nile. She saw me.

Her head turned briefly, dark eyes on mine for an instant, and then she looked ahead again. I kept my car even with hers until we reached the street by the bay, reached the house where I had slept last night.

Nile parked her car and got out. I stopped my car

behind Nile's and we walked toward each other. She looked at me, a strange searching of her eyes on my face.

"Black wasn't right, Nile."

"He wasn't?"

"The truth is what I told you on the phone this morning."

"Are there pictures of us — of us together?"

"Yes. I didn't know they were taken until after I'd called you."

"You know the man who took them?"

"Yes."

"Why did Ringling call you a blackmailer?"

"Because that's what I came to Balboa to do. I changed my mind — hell, I changed my life this morning. Because of you, Nile."

"And the pictures?"

"I'll get them, destroy them. I swear it, Nile."

"It isn't necessary, Bill. The pictures mean nothing to me, I'm not ashamed.

"I told that to Ringling when he called. I'm a grown woman, without a man."

She was close to me, a small woman, looking up. "I don't care what people know about me. I might pretend to worry, but the truth is that I don't care. I'm not John Lisbon's wife now. Show your dirty pictures where you want to. I'm not ashamed of what I've done."

There was anger, a lava burst of anger behind the dark eyes. She slapped me hard and turned away. I took her by the arms, swung her to me.

"Nile. I love you."

"You've loved a lot of women. Where are they now?"

"Remember what we talked about this morning,

Nile? Those things were true."

She tried to pull herself away from me.

"And while you were telling me those things your partner was developing his pictures."

"You say you don't care about those."

This was fury now. Her face was close to mine. "I'm not ashamed of what I've done. I'm ashamed of you, ashamed that I thought you were a man. A woman has a man, strong, wise, a lover. He dies and she tries to find a man again — not only a lover, but a man with strength in himself, a complete man. There are damn few of them and you aren't one."

She pulled back, her arms free, and she stood, breasts thrust high, hands on her hips. "Maybe it's not hard to get a lonely woman into bed, maybe it isn't much trouble to make her forget that she's lonely for that time. Most men want to try it — and then when they've done their little tricks, told their sweet little lies, shown that they are males, then what? Then it's nothing, Oxford, it's always nothing more. I thought you had something more, and I was right. You had a scheme, a scheme to force Ringling Black through me.

"Black's got more decency and strength in his finger than your whole damn family's had since the first of them was whelped in a dung pile. Do you understand me?"

She walked to the door, took her key from her purse, and unlocked it. As the door opened my arm was around her, and I pushed her inside, closing it behind us.

She fought me, scratching, kicking, butting at me with the glossy hair flying as her head came up under my chin. I fought to hold her first, brought up her mouth as my hand forced her chin, kissed her. She tried to bite at my face and she reached for the shoe on her right foot, her knee high. I slapped the shoe out of her hand, kissed her again and suddenly it was as it had been this morning.

It was strange, and terrible too, because we were lovers whipped by forces that were not love. For me it was something that I had to do now that everything else was lost, like a savage warrior being with his woman before he goes into a battle in which he will be destroyed. I don't know what it was for her. If it was love, it was a cruel typhoon of nerve, muscle, and flesh.

We were looking at each other, without words. It was over, and we did not know what our world was for us now. It had changed, and we did not yet know what our lives would be after this.

The front door opened and I turned. King McCarthy was standing there looking at us, looking at Nile's clothes and the bloody scratches on my face.

I was standing by the time he got to me, standing as a solid target for the left fist that knocked me over a chair.

He was coming for me, fast, and I pushed the chair up between us, the legs blocking his arms. I tried to lift it higher to use it as an awkward club to beat at his head, and he pulled it away from me. I kicked at him as he twisted his body and then he got me with both fists against my body, rib-bending blows that took my strength as if my lungs had exploded.

I dug my head under his chin and tried to hit him in the stomach. He pushed me away with a left and brought the right up. I caught it at the corner of my mouth and cheek, like the kick of a horse. Again I went over backward, arms out, hitting the floor hard with my spine and head.

"Kill him, King! Kick him to death!"

I heard that and I waited for the truck driver's boots to stomp me.

McCarthy stood above me. I could see his face, the white teeth showing in the death-fight grin, leather jacket hanging open from the khaki shirt, the tight black curls of hair over the tanned face and the glittering eyes. He looked at me and then he turned to Nile, lifted her, and took her in his arms. King wasn't done with me yet, but he could come back for the unfinished business later.

Neither of them saw me as I pulled myself up, hurting and weak. They were looking at each other when I took the lamp from the hall table and hit McCarthy on the back of the head. Maybe he turned a little just before the lamp shattered against the black hair that touched the back of his collar. It was a heavy pottery lamp. He fell against Nile and they both went down. She screamed. McCarthy made no sound except the thump of his body rolling away from her to the floor.

Maybe he would have killed me in the next few seconds if I had not done it. I do not know.

Nile was bending over him now. I guess some time had passed, possibly a minute or longer. I went to the door, still half open, walked out, pushing it closed behind me. It wasn't easy to walk to my car. McCarthy had hurt me, and the pains were only beginning to start. I got behind the wheel, fumbled a little, and got it moving. Black had hit me, and fairly solidly, but McCarthy had brutal power in his hard fists. I wanted to crawl into someplace dark, cool, and soft.

Instead I had to move. One thought cut through the

pain fog and the frantic desperation: I love her, I love her no matter what. I know what love is now — and it's not all good, not all kind, not all forgiving. But I love Nile Lisbon, no matter what.

I could still hear her voice, husky, saying, "Kill him, King! Kick him to death!" but it wasn't important. Maybe I knew how she had felt and I didn't blame her.

My face and head hurt bad. Cool water might help. I drove, clumsily, toward the Inn.

There were a few people in the lobby, most of them under twenty-three. My swollen face and bruised mouth rated some attention, a laugh or two and smiles. It wasn't funny to me. As I opened the door to my room I stopped thinking about my pains and began to think about murder.

Several kinds of murder. For the first time I realized that I might have killed King McCarthy. The lamp was heavy enough and I'd caught him at the base of the skull with a pretty fair swing. The thought was like having the bottom of my belly drop out.

As quickly as I saw McCarthy dead, the dark blood puddling around the leather jacket, I had another vivid mental picture. McCarthy alive, with a bad headache maybe, but alive. Alive and with one purpose in life — finding and killing Bill Oxford. As he saw it, he had plenty of reason.

Nile and me there, just beyond the entrance, the fresh bleeding scratches on my face, Nile screaming at him to kill me ... I knew the kind of man King McCarthy was, and that's the kind of man who would hunt me down and tear me apart with his hands. I could be guarded by an armored division and hide in a vault at Fort Knox, but McCarthy would get to me.

For good reasons, as he saw it.

O.K., Oxford, I thought as I held onto the lavatory basin and looked at myself in the mirror above it. Fix yourself out of this one, fixer.

I wasn't afraid, but it was a hell of an odd feeling.

My face looked no good. Three long scratches, the blood still coming out in tiny beads. One corner of my upper lip swelling into something that felt like a golf ball. A few shattered small bruises. Down below my ribs ached individually.

I stripped down and went to work with hot water, cold water, alcohol, and towels. Cold shower, cold packs, warm tub, cold shower again.

In the tub I waited for the knock on the door with the Newport police behind the knock. If you've got to wait for something, that isn't the best thing — listening as people walk along the corridor in front of your door, thinking they were stopping, waiting for them to knock and say, "Oxford, this is the police. We want you — for murder." But I had to have the tub, I had to get into some kind of shape, because I was staying in Balboa until I'd played this trick out.

No running. Not from a hate-crazed guy in a leather jacket, not from a tall, soft-spoken lawyer whose eyes bit into me with contempt, not from a pretty girl whose life I'd kicked into the trash pile casually and carelessly, not from a small woman who might hate me and might love me both, not from the police. Just not running.

I had fresh clothes on and I was wondering what to do about the scratches when the room phone rang.

Well, it won't be a friend that's calling, I thought as I picked it up.

It wasn't any friend, it was the big man in Los

Angeles. This time his voice was harsh.

"What's going on down there, Oxford?"

"Why?"

"You know I can't talk real plain over the phone. That fellow Harry called me a little while ago. He says that jerk in Balboa — you know who I mean — has got television time arranged for tonight and he's going to blow the lid right off."

"I guess that's right."

"You guess? You know how important this thing is to us? We've spent sixty thousand bucks for billboard space alone for our man — nearly three hundred thousand so far for everything. We aren't figuring on losing just because some hick lawyer with a bug on his tail spills a lot of stuff in front of the goddamn public on a television spot! You went down there to stop that guy and instead of stopping him you've got him hot to go. What the hell are you doing?"

"Can't you use pressure on the television station?"

"For the last half hour I've been trying to use pressure. The station won't back down. The state committee bought the time and this lawyer is going to use it tonight instead of some spellbinder they had lined up. If Black shows that stuff tonight, we lose the primary and we can kiss off about fifty millions. This isn't going to happen, you understand?"

"It's out of my hands."

"If you can't produce, we'll use other means. Any means. And if you don't produce before that telecast tonight, you're going to wish your mother had strangled you at birth, because my crowd is plenty sore, and when we're sore somebody pays. Either produce or we'll bury you in San Quentin in solitary for a stretch that won't quit. You got it straight,

Oxford? You produce, and you produce goddam fast!"

The phone clicked.

For a man hesitant about talking over a phone, the big man had said quite a bit. It came out short and simple: Whether I produced or not, Ringling Black would not tell the repulsive truth about their candidate on TV tonight, if they had to kill him to stop him. And if I wasn't the man who stopped him, they were angry enough to make Oxford an example to the rest of their dirty-trick boys, showing what happened to a fixer who didn't fix. It was really simple and direct, what the man had said.

I knotted a tie, took another look at my face, and left my room. At least the police hadn't come. In the shadowy bar downstairs I had one drink. It tasted good all the way down. The bar was beginning to crowd up with men and girls in their early twenties, almost all of them already in swim clothes.

Balboa isn't big. If somebody is looking for you, you can't be too hard to find.

The question right now concerned one more drink. I wanted one more, I wanted to stay in the shadowy bar listening to the kids around me, watching them smile at each other, girls with smooth, long legs, boys with young faces. It wasn't indecision that made me stay on the bar stool; I knew what I would have to do.

Two things: I would phone Nile Lisbon and find out what had happened to King; I would find Black again and get on his team — if he would let me. He was going to need me.

"Another shot, please," I called to the barman. What I said to myself was: You really hate to go out and face it, don't you, Oxford? The barman put the drink in front of me and I paid for it, then I got up and walked out, leaving it untouched on the bar. It may have looked odd, but then, lots of odd things happen at bars.

I went into the phone booth and called Nile Lisbon's home.

"Hello?" Her voice, soft, low.

"This is Bill Oxford."

"Good Lord!" This was almost a whisper.

I waited.

"Where are you?"

"A phone booth at the Inn."

"I thought you would go back to Los Angeles. He's looking for you."

"How is he?"

"Crazy mad."

"What did you tell him?"

"He was out for about five minutes. When he came to I couldn't keep him in the house. His head isn't cut much, but there's a big lump." Her voice was still a husky whisper.

"What kind of car is he driving?"

"Mine. He doesn't have one."

"How long have you and he — "

"Does that matter?"

I thought about that. "It matters, but maybe not right now. Nile, I didn't lie to you. I played it straight last night with you. I'm playing it straight with everybody now. You, Black, everybody."

"Get out of town, Bill. Get out of town. I know what King can be like when he's crazy angry. Get out of town."

"I'm staying."

"He'll find you. He's not the smartest guy in the world, I know that. But he'll find you."

"Nile, call Ringling Black. Ask him to come to your place right away."

"Why?"

"I have to see him. It's more important than anything else that I see Ringling Black right away. After that your boy can find me, or the cops can pick me up, or anything. But it's life or death to Black that I see him right away."

"You're lying." The voice was higher now, not shrill, but not soft and husky.

"Believe me if you will ever believe me, Nile. I know what they'll do to Black. Call him. I'll be at your house in ten minutes."

I hung up on her as she was saying, "No."

It's usually difficult to be the brave knight on the white horse fighting the powers of evil to protect the good and the innocent when the good ones think you're a heel or a rat.

If anybody in this deal was good or innocent. Maybe Ringling Black was, but he'd be kind of lonely.

CHAPTER TEN

One thing I knew and understood — the big men in Los Angeles meant what they threatened. They had to stop Ringling Black before he showed his stuff on the telecast tonight.

The five thousand dollars that had been my fee for stopping Black wasn't important money to them. Even the three hundred thousand dollars the primary campaign for their candidate had cost them to date wasn't too important. But the fifty millions or more that his election would mean was damned important.

Once their man was in, it wouldn't be graft, or gambling, or any of the obvious things. He would appoint certain men to certain jobs, he would help push through minor changes in a few laws, he would handle the enforcement of other laws.

The result would be that the big men would gain control of the empire of California. The laws that hampered them would not be enforced, the laws that hamstrung their competition would be pushed until the competitors screamed for mercy and sold out. The oil would flow, the big transport trucks would roll, the thousands of liquor stores would tinkle with the sound of their cash registers, the housewives would trundle the grocery carts past the cashiers in the supermarkets, and the whole damn thing would pay the big men a penny more here, a penny less in taxes there, and it would add to million upon million each year.

If their candidate got in.

One dead Ringling Black wouldn't tip the scales against fifty million dollars.

I got in my car and my ribs moaned a little.

Bay Avenue, the three-block main street of Balboa, was bubbling with kids and cars now. It was slow moving.

Ann Field was turning the corner of Bay and Central. I swung my car into a spot with a sign that said "No Parking" and jumped out. We met almost face to face.

Her face went tight with fear for an instant, and then her chin rose a little and her shoulders went back.

"Ann!"

"Get away from me, you son-of-a-bitch. Get away.

I'm through with you and your slimy kind."

"You did right, Ann. I'm glad you told Black."

She smiled bitterly. "Sure. And now you want me to get in your car and meet some friends of yours. Nice friends that will knock my teeth out and break my nose?"

"This is straight, Ann. You were right. I went to Black myself to tell him about the deal — after you'd been there. I'm through with the slime, too."

Her eyes searched mine, and then the stiffness went out of her body. One hand touched my arm.

"You mean that, Bill? You aren't lying to me?"

"I walked along the beach this morning, Ann. There was a sickness in me and I was alone with it, looking into myself. Maybe it sounds foolish, crazy — but I had to change, and change fast."

Ann looked away, her lips tight.

"You liked me once, Ann. What did you like about me?"

"Liked you? I loved you. You were a proud, happy guy. It was fun just to see your eyes and your smile. You were a kid that wasn't afraid of the world, you loved the world, and you were going to do great. Do great and have fun doing it. A girl could feel it."

"The kid is dead. But I'm going to try to be a man. It won't be easy, maybe I've forgotten how, and the things I'll have to do won't make much sense, not to me or to anybody else. But I have to do them."

"What kind of things, Bill?"

"I came here to do a slimy job. Just running out on it won't be enough. I've got to go the other way — help the man I was supposed to destroy."

Ann was looking into my eyes.

"That's why I came here to Balboa, Bill. To try to

find something left inside me that was still clean, still young and good. But the first thing I did was get drunk."

"You did something that took courage today, Ann. You'll come through."

"Do you mean that, Bill?"

"I mean it."

"Lord, how many men I've said those words to, and how many have given me that answer! They all lied." Her face was suddenly tired and old, without hope. Yet she was still a young and beautiful girl. The boys who passed us looked at her with young men's approval.

"It's been a lousy life, Ann. It's damned near ruined both of us. I'm through with it. I'll help you in every way I can — but I'm going to be hot now, too. Don't you worry, nobody knows that you crossed me. Nobody will."

The searching eyes and then she smiled. It was almost the Ann Field smile of six long years ago.

"You are being straight." Her hand was tight on my arm. She kissed me, standing in the fog-streaked afternoon sunlight on the corner of Bay and Central while the beautiful laughing kids walked by us and the jukeboxes jingled from the doorways. "Six years, Bill. Six dirty years down the sewer."

The kiss was a surprise, but I could see that her eyes were soft again and her face different. It looked as it had when I first knew Ann Field.

"I had to do that this morning, Bill. I left you and I was sick of myself and what you and I had turned into. Do you think I'd make a good telephone operator or salesgirl or something, Bill?"

"Sure, kid. And I'll make a good car salesman or

maybe a mechanic. I was good with tools when I was a boy."

It was a foolish conversation. Both of us knew what we had each discovered today, and it must have been something like getting religion.

"Where are you going to stay, Ann? It'll be impossible to get a room in this town."

"I'm going back to Los Angeles, move in with my folks, and start looking for a job." Her hand was on my arm, and she was looking at me as a child might — hopeful, a little timid. "Would you want to see me maybe sometime? We could go swimming, or maybe to a movie or something."

Somewhere back in the early years Ann Field must really have fallen a little bit in love with Bill Oxford, and it must have stayed with her, sometimes as love and sometimes as hate, but she had not lost it.

"It sounds good to me, Ann."

Briefly there in the spring sunlight we felt a closeness, as if we were the kids of an Easter week in Balboa six years ago, kids who liked each other.

"I've got fish to fry, Ann."

"You mean that about seeing me? We could have fun, Bill."

"What's the name of the hotel where your folks are staying?"

"The Pendleton. It isn't much. But I'll be better off with my folks."

"I'll call you at the Pendleton. So long, Ann."

"I'll be waiting, Bill."

I knew I was making the same mistake that I must have made six years ago, but how could I help it?

"Can I drive you any place?" I called back. She was still standing there, looking at me.

"No. I'll just walk around until it's time for my bus. 'By, Bill."

I got into my car and drove out towards Nile Lisbon's house. For a little time I forgot the big men, forgot King McCarthy, even forgot Nile Lisbon. I was thinking about Ann. It's a brutal world that will wreck something as fine as that girl, and it's good to see her essential fineness show through as strength.

Nile's car wasn't in front of her house. That meant King McCarthy was somewhere in Balboa, hunting me. There would be quite a few people hunting me soon, including about four thousand bucks' worth of creditors. I thought of something about "paying the piper" as I got out of the Mercury and walked once more toward the front door of Nile Lisbon's home.

The door was unlocked and I pushed it open. Ringling Black was coming down the stairway.

"Get it straight," I said to him. "Whatever else may be true, I'm here to help you make that telecast tonight."

He stopped, not quite at the bottom of the stairs, and looked down at me.

"What you mean, Oxford, is that you are here to stop me at any cost. I made you a promise today and I'm going to keep it. Wherever I see you I'm going to knock you into the gutter until you get out of this town. I'm going to do it now.

My face and body had taken too much punishment for me to take any more. I picked up the chair that I had used against McCarthy.

"I'm here to maybe save your life, Black. If I have to slug you to do it, I will."

Nile came from the second floor to the head of the stairway.

"Let him talk, Ring. I'm dead sick of trouble in this house. Let him talk and let him go." She was looking at me as she spoke, her dark eyes hot.

"Say whatever you have to say, Oxford."

I put the chair down. "I came here to Balboa to frame you. I was going to use that girl, Ann Field, and then I was going to make a bargain with you for your evidence. That's all true — and that's all over."

"How about the pictures of you and — " He couldn't finish the sentence.

"I'm in love with Nile. Whatever we did last night we did. Harry Podden is a private detective, a cheap little divorce-evidence shyster. He's working for the same people that sent me here. He's still working for them. I am not. I didn't know he had the pictures and if I have to break his neck to get them and destroy them I will."

"The pictures aren't important. I told you that," said Nile.

"Mrs. Lisbon is sometimes the victim of her situation," said Ringling Black. "Her friends know and understand. To put it simply, she has a powerful and overwhelming need for love, and her standards for complete love have been too high for her to find one right man. I know that. Like her other old, close friends, I will do everything to protect her from men like you."

Nile came down the stairs, passing Black. She stood in front of me, a small woman, her shadowed eyes opened wide.

"I've been fooling myself for a long time, since a little while after John died. I guess I have to stop fooling myself now. Ring, you know what there is to know about me, and you know that you and I don't —

haven't — that we aren't — "

Black stepped down to her, put his arm around her shoulders. "I know. But let's not talk about private things in front of this stranger."

"Stranger?" Nile asked, with a small smile.

Black dropped his arm. "You're cruel sometimes, Nile."

Nile looked up at me. "You talk of love very easily, Bill Oxford."

I was understanding, a little, why King McCarthy and Ringling Black had looked at me with that strange pity. Nile Lisbon had charm, and a man could sense the whirlpool, the power that drew you in beyond that compelling charm, into a wild storm. When you had known that, you were hers. And when you were hers, she went on, searching for a more complete man.

"I do not talk of love very easily, Nile Lisbon," I said.

"It's odd," she said softly. "Ring was the first, and you are the last."

I could feel the ruthless edge of cruelty in Nile, and I knew that cruelty was part of her strength.

"Black, the men who hired me for that job phoned me a little while ago. They told me they would use any means to stop you making the telecast."

"Let them try."

"Do you know how powerful these people are? Do you realize what this election means to them?"

"I know them. They don't frighten me. They're trying to elect a crook and a criminal into power so they can bleed California. I'm going to expose him tonight and they aren't going to stop me."

"Then go into hiding. Get out of Balboa and keep a bodyguard around you until you get in front of the TV cameras tonight. If you don't, they'll get you."

"Who's the bodyguard, you?" His mouth was twisted with contempt.

"You could find worse."

"For getting out of town, Bill, you might think of yourself. If you stay here, King will find you. He'll kill you, Bill." Nile was intent, her mouth pleading.

Black looked at her in surprise. "King? You mean that driver who is always getting into trouble? King McCarthy?"

"He's been the most important, Ring. I'm sorry."

Black looked sick, and his shoulders slumped a little. Both of us, there at the foot of the stairs in Nile Lisbon's house, loved her. I wondered, at that moment, how much of our love for her was formed by the violence of her need and by the challenge of her dissatisfaction. Nile was a challenge to each man she met, not to seduce her, but to hold her after the knowing of the whirlpool and the typhoon. If it is not love, it has the quality of love.

"It's your life, Nile." Black looked away. The first one, the first one to know the whirlpool after John Lisbon had died, the first one to fail the basic challenge Nile Lisbon had made to his maleness and his completeness.

"Do you want me to help you until you make your telecast?" I asked. I wanted to get out of this house, get away, I wanted a drink.

"No. Maybe you're telling the truth now, Oxford, and maybe you're still working for the bunch that sent you here. I don't know and I don't care. I want no part of you. And I'm making that telecast tonight, over the Rockwood network at nine."

I went to the door. There was a chill over me as if I were talking to a dead man.

"O.K. Good-by, Nile."

"Bill, do you understand why I screamed at King to kill you? If you do, you understand me better than I do myself." Nile stood at the door, next to me.

"Good-by, Nile."

I pulled the door closed behind me. At least I had told Ringling Black. I was square with that part of it. Now I could go back to my own worries.

The Mercury moved out and away from the house. Where to? Good question, Bill. Where do you go from here?

Nile Lisbon. Haunted, searching, demanding, rejecting, violent, warm, giving full contentment and giving none. A woman whose charm bound a man like soft chains, and yet a lonely woman in hell. There was nothing that had happened that made me love her less than I had at dawn this morning, and yet I knew so much more.

A man cannot walk away from this and go to another woman with pride and sureness. There was a challenge and he had failed, he was not complete enough as a man. Maybe the great women, the famous women, were something like Nile. We remember best the women who were not wives, but women who challenged men to be their lovers.

I swung along Central and my car was bumper to bumper in a column of cars, the first full flood of the Easter-week crowds.

In mid-block I saw them on the sidewalk, talking together as they went along. Ann Field and Harry Podden, walking closely together.

Traffic was too heavy; I couldn't swing off Central until the next block, and by the time I had circled back they were gone. Ann Field and Harry Podden.

CHAPTER ELEVEN

The only parking spaces downtown were along the ocean front near the Rendezvous ballroom. I slammed my car into one of them and double-timed back toward Bay and Central. Podden was poison and Ann couldn't take much more of that kind of poison. I wanted to find them, and quick.

As I passed the patio entrance to the Inn I stopped. The big guns were moving in on the situation, and one of the biggest and smoothest was coming out of the Inn. Roger Mooney, vice-president of the West Coast division of the advertising agency, saw me and waved. I had to stop. This was the man who had been my boss.

"Hi, Bill! Looking for you boy." He glanced at my face, looked away, and held out his hand. Of course he had seen the scratches and the bruises, and his mind was a cash register: Is Oxford making money for the agency or is he running a debit for the agency? In the next minute or two he'd find out how I got those scratches and bruises, and decide the profit or loss value to the agency. To Roger Mooney nothing else mattered, and everything that happened had to be assessed in those terms.

"Hello, Roger." We shook hands.

"Have a little trouble, Bill?" Mooney did not look like what he was. He was a youthful forty, slender, blue-eyed, smiling. Until you knew him a little, you might figure him for one hell of a good-natured guy, open and friendly. It would be like mistaking a twenty-foot killer shark for a porpoise.

"Yeah, a fight."

"Concerned with this matter you're attending to here?" Mooney was smiling, as if his questions weren't important and as if it didn't matter much how I answered. I knew damn well that his brain had a kind of tape recorder in it, and the recorder was spinning now.

Every word I said would be examined for meaning, for the tone, for the length of pause, examined, analyzed, and run through the cash register. A year from now he would remember what I had said, and exactly how I had said it.

"No. Private matter."

"Is that good judgment, Bill?" Pleasant, smiling face, bright blue eyes. But that was the phrase Roger Mooney used as a red alert — meaning that you were doing something that wasn't making money for the agency.

"I'm bugging out, Mooney." That was it now. Calling him by his last name was the same signal to him it would be for me if he called me "Oxford"—the end.

"I'm sorry, Bill. I don't understand the phrase." The smile rippled, and he put an arm around my shoulders. "Let's go in and have a quick one while you brief me on the picture here. I'm afraid I'm a little out of focus on it."

My chances of finding Podden and Ann would still be good, but this was one of the top guns. Mooney's coming to Balboa in person meant that hell was popping in Los Angeles.

"I'll have a drink with you." Once I had thought I would like to be a kind of Roger Mooney, fifty thousand a year, pieces of a lot of the good solid deals that came up, and expense account that made a monkey out of income taxes — and power, lots of power.

Later I realized that I'd live to dance on his grave. One day, in a month, in a couple of years, the blue eyes would stare and the smile would freeze, and the bursting heart would rip. For each fifty thousand in annual salary Roger Mooney paid with five years of normal life.

We went into the cool saloon of the Inn and sat in a booth. Mooney ordered a rye Old-Fashioned; I had a straight shot of sour-mash whisky.

"Sketch things in for me, Bill." Mooney leaned forward, cocking his head like a listening bird.

"Ringling Black won't scare and he won't bargain. He's going to make a telecast tonight and show the evidence against this joker of a candidate. That's it."

Mooney grimaced, tasted his drink, looked at it for a moment, and then moved his head forward again. "Some important people have put a lot of confidence in you, Bill, and you know what this thing means to the agency."

"That's the way it is. I won't frame the man, and if I did, he wouldn't back down. As near as I can judge, Ringling Black is smart and honest, with guts."

"As you know, Bill, neither the agency nor I care to know details on these special jobs you do. I assume you'd have a conference with this fellow Black and straighten everything out. Beyond that we're not concerned with details."

"Then I'll sketch you the picture, I'll brief you, and I'll put things into focus for you. I've been working in a sewer for the agency. I've done things just this side of murder, and the only difference between me and a Main Street pimp is that he associates with nicer people. This deal on Black was the new low — jam up a decent guy so that the voters of California will put in a man I wouldn't trust with an eight-year-old girl or a March of Dimes collection box. I've finally got sick of my job. Are you sketched in? Are you briefed? Are you in focus?"

"Apparently, Oxford, you've been involved in matters that the agency has not been aware of, or could possibly condone. Needless to say, this shows non-co-operation on your part, and the agency will not tolerate non-co-operation. Effective at once, you have left the agency. We'll send you written confirmation of this, with your final check, and the trade papers will be notified."

He stood up. "You have been an employee of the agency, Oxford, and it is in the best interests of the agency that you should not be involved in immediate trouble, so I would suggest that you leave California at once. I happen to know that several warrants for your arrest will be issued this afternoon."

Mooney walked away, a slender little guy whose strained heart would rip someday. He left the check for me to pay, and naturally it was done deliberately. The agency expense accounts were no longer for Bill Oxford.

It was worth the five minutes. I had accomplished several things. Mooney was here to mastermind operations and I had heard agency gossip that Mooney had used hired killers where it had been necessary years ago. California had been a rough state in the late 1930's. The chips were down for Mooney today. He had to keep Ringling Black from making that telecast. No excuses.

Also these five minutes had given me a chance to resign formally, so to speak, from my position with the agency. I was a free man now, until the cops caught up with me.

I paid the check and went out, down Bay, over on Central. There were crowds, but I did not see Ann or the private detective. The bars, three of them, were filled with singing kids, but no Ann, no Podden.

Sooner or later, I thought, McCarthy and I will run into each other. Then there will be a senseless, bloody fight with no good in it for anyone, least of all for Nile.

Lovely woman in hell. Maybe now I could understand her a little, but understanding wasn't freedom from passion. Men will kill, leave their families, embezzle, commit suicide for some women, and for lovelier and finer women they will be selfish and casual. Hard to figure, but I knew that Nile was the first kind, as Ann was the second. Ringling Black knowing Nile for what she was, was still in love with her, wanted to marry her, bound by the charm and the whirlpool.

There are only a few such women, but they move through many lives like typhoons. I wondered, now, about her marriage to John Lisbon. Had he tamed the typhoon, or did he die trying?

I could think about these things and it did no good; I knew that my life was knotted into Nile's.

There were rabbits and eggs as decorations for the stores along Central, ancient symbols of a pagan Easter ten thousand years before there was the Christ. The handsome kids strode by, and I wondered how many of the ten thousand knew consciously that these nine days were no ordinary vacation with the gang, no simple prolonged beach and house party. These were the days of the wonderful and terrible rites of spring, the fertility feast, ancient, pagan.

The girls knew, I think. I could remember confidences from girls at Balboa, and they knew the real meaning of these nine days, more than laughter, more than sports cars and dancing to Kenton or Brubeck, much more — strange, terrible, needed.

The street was crowded all the way to the pavilion at the end of Bay, and the short beach was filled with moving, talking, laughing groups of kids. An odd thing about this beach along the bay in Easter week — compared to Jones Beach or Oak Street in Chicago, or Santa Monica, this was a tightly policed crowd. Not policed by older people; if they'd been around, the discipline of the groups would have fallen apart. These kids policed themselves, naturally and unconsciously. The overloud nuisance of a guy wasn't wanted by his crowd, the bitchy girl wasn't wanted by her crowd. To get along during the nine days at Balboa, the boy and the girl had to conform, and conform to curiously different and stricter standards than ordinary society imposed.

I was out of place, too old, wearing a suit rather than swimming trunks, alone instead of being with a crowd. I walked back to Bay and Central. Another drink would taste damn fine, another few minutes in a cool, dark bar would be damn comfortable.

Then I saw Harry Podden in the crowd, a hurrying, nervous man. He felt my fingers bite into his shoulder as I caught up with him, and he seemed to squeak as he turned his head to look at me.

By good luck I saw the Newport police squad car cruising slowly across the street. If I smashed Podden down it would be the end of the chapter for me right now, and maybe the end of a book. The warrants would be out this afternoon, Roger Mooney had said.

"I want those pictures and negatives," I said, my fingers hard into his shoulder.

"O.K., O.K., I made a mistake, I'm sorry, don't cause trouble!"

"Where are they?"

"In my car, down on the lot. Please don't start any trouble."

"Let's go."

We walked down Bay to the big lot between Balboa pier and the Rendezvous. Neither of us said anything. Harry Podden's car was old and badly used. He opened the door, took out a brief case, and pulled out a Manila envelope.

"Here they are. It seemed like a good idea." Podden was watching me, the sweat shiny on his face.

I looked at the prints, checked the negatives. Podden's infrared photography had been good, too good. Looking at these pictures brought back the excitement that I had known before dawn this morning. I could have killed Podden for having dared to see this, and then my hands unclenched. As Nile had said, the pictures didn't matter.

They could have cost her her reputation, her secure position in the county society, her job as an assistant district attorney, but these things didn't matter to her. The typhoon of her emotions was not concerned with the weather reports of the people around her. I could guess that those things had been saved for her, not by lies of pretense on her part, but by the lies and pretense of her friends, protecting her. Nile would lie, of course, but only to men and for men's reasons.

My lighter flamed in my hands, the pictures and the negatives curled into ashes.

"You know how it is in my business," mumbled

Podden. "That stuff ain't new to me. I don't hardly notice the pictures I take. I've shot hundreds, maybe, like that."

"What were you doing with Ann Field a few minutes ago?"

"Who?" Podden was sweating again.

"Ann Field. The girl you saw with me last night."

"Oh, her."

"Talk, Podden."

He knew what I meant. We were alone among the long rows of parked cars. A hundred yards away the pacific rollers were booming into the surge of the surf.

"I was just asking her if she knew where I could find you."

Poor Podden. Even his lies were clumsy and weak. I felt sorry for the little boy, and the snuffling girl on Linden Avenue. I slapped him and he reeled against the dusty rust of his car.

"Don't get rough, Oxford. You ain't so much any more. You're through, big shot!"

"That's right. Now get it out about this girl — quick and level!" I moved forward on him.

"No! Please, I got a bad heart. I could maybe die." His hands, palms facing me, were up. "I'm still trying to make the score on this deal. I need the money, my kids are sick."

I didn't say anything.

"You can look at this girl and see what she is, maybe not quite a hustler yet, but she's been around plenty. I was trying to figure a shot on this deal and I saw her."

"What did you tell her?"

"Nothing, nothing. Just talking. Trying to figure using her maybe in a shot at this Black. He don't give much under pressure, does he? What a jerk!"

"He's a jerk?"

"Sure he's a jerk. He can't win, you know that, you've been around. You know the guys we're working for, they won't be bothered with no guy like Black. In case you don't know, Oxford, I'm top man in this caper now. I talked to L.A. and I'm the guy they're depending upon."

Harry Podden, still hoping. Roger Mooney was in town, and Roger would have his connections either here or racing along the Santa Ana freeway toward Newport in their Cadillacs. Oxford and Podden had messed this deal up, and time was shortening to the time of Black's telecast, which would dump three hundred thousand dollars of campaign expenses and maybe fifty million in loot down the drain.

"Yeah, Oxford. Get that — I'm top man. I talked to L.A., to the wheels." He was gaining courage, mopping the sweat from his face with his sleeve.

"What did this girl tell you?"

"Nothing. She seems to think you're a great guy."

"She was talking about killing me last night," I said, half to myself.

"You're kidding. She tells me what a great guy you are. She's really gone on you, Oxford. Of course," he winked, "you're a real make-out artist, aren't you? You sure get a lot, don't you?"

I started to walk away. Podden would lie and there'd be no truth I could get except by beating him. The best thing would be to get away from him.

"This one looks kinda trampish, no offense. She thinks you're great, but her — she's got that tramp look, you know what I mean?

Maybe Podden was one of those strange men that like to be hit. Maybe that's why he got into a business where he was begging for a beating almost every working day. I didn't hit him, I walked away.

"Just remember, Oxford, I'm top man. I'm running things."

I was fifty feet away from him when I saw the squad car cruising between the parking lines. The officer on the right was checking licenses. When he saw Podden's tags he spoke to the driver and the car stopped. I stepped back beyond the next row.

Podden had seen the police car. He slammed the door of his own car and began to walk away.

"Hey, you!"

Podden turned. Both police officers were up to him now.

"Your name Podden, Harry Podden?"

"Yeah. Why?"

"We got a pickup order on you. Come along, fella."

"What's the idea? What pickup? I'm licensed. Here's my — "

"Vagrancy. Maybe more stuff. Come along."

Harry tried to squirm and the smaller cop hit him on the jaw. Podden sagged into the arms of the two policemen and they dragged him to their car. I watched them drive away.

I could guess that Roger Mooney was in action, clearing the deck of the men in his way. I could guess, too, that there'd be a pick-up order for Bill Oxford damn soon.

For me it would be only the beginning. If I knew the ticket for me, it would be punched clear to the gray walls of San Quentin above the fog-dull waters of the bay near San Francisco. Nothing personal, just the way guys like me got handled when they didn't produce.

CHAPTER TWELVE

I got into my car and drove back to Newport, two miles back along the narrow sandy peninsula. Some of the houses along Central had signs up now, "U.C.L.A. Castle," "Hollywood Hi Zortch Society," "The Beat Club," "Fremont Fun House," and a dozen more. It was part of Easter week, plastering the rented summer homes with gaudy signs. Most of the windows, and usually the front doors, were open, with the music spilling out across the traffic on Central. This was late Friday afternoon; tonight would be the first big night.

The Pacific Electric bus depot was a weathered old building half a dozen blocks beyond the little business section of Newport. I hoped to find Ann there, waiting for the big red bus that would take her the forty miles north to Los Angeles. Ann wasn't around the depot so I sat down on a bench inside. The bus was due in about thirty minutes.

Going to sleep is something I don't remember. But it was nearly three hours later when I woke up, stiff and cold. After I woke up I felt stupid, but it had figured — lots of drinking, no food, little sleep, and enough emotional kicks through the day to keep me going until I sat on that damn bench.

Apparently nobody had bothered me, sprawled along the slatted bench. Ann might have come and gone without seeing me. I rubbed my face, still sore, and worked my arms. I was plenty hungry now. You don't slide into gear quickly after you wake up that way, and I felt that the inside of my head was lined with long fuzz.

One idea cut through the fuzz — go to Christian's Hut and get a good meal. A man isn't worth much without food inside. It took ten minutes to drive to Christian's and the parking lot was almost filled. It was cocktail time now, and the bar with the window overlooking the lovely bay was busy.

The first drink tasted fine. I wondered if the pickup order was out on me. Probably. Roger Mooney always did what had to be done right fast.

"Guy was in here looking for you a couple of times," said the barman. "I think it was you. Described you and said your name was Oxford. Guy in a leather jacket."

"Thanks," I said. "I'll have another." I could hear sirens somewhere near.

The bay was darkening, and the white hulls of the boats were startlingly bright against the purple-gray water. After the second drink I went upstairs and had me a great big steak. It hurt a little to work my jaws, but the steak was worth the trouble. I followed it with some winy-rich coffee and a double pony of brandy.

O.K., world, I thought, turn your dogs loose on me. I'm ready. Now the urge was with me to see Nile Lisbon, to be with her. It wasn't a frantic urge for the violence of the whirlpool; this was a need to be with the woman quietly, to sit somewhere with her, maybe talking, maybe silent. I wanted to sense her charm again, to look into the shadow-black eyes. I went to the phone.

Nile's phone rang for more than a minute before I hung up the receiver and heard my dime tinkle back. I felt lonely, like a guy at the end of the world. What I didn't want to do was sit through the evening at the bar, drinking, telephoning every few minutes, waiting until at last Nile Lisbon was home and I was stupid drunk again.

But that's the way I started the evening at the bar, phoning between drinks. Three drinks, and three times the dime jingled into the return slot. Christian's is a hard place to leave, especially when you have no other place to go. It seems somewhat like a little island in a halfway heaven, with the golden shoulders and legs of pretty girls, the strumming of the island music, the ghost yachts in the twilight on the bay, and nothing real. But somewhere near was a scream of sirens.

For the fourth time since dinner I dialed the Lisbon number, listened to the ringing, hung up, and picked my dime out of the slot. When I went back to the bar Whitey D'Arcy was standing in the doorway and it turned out he was looking for me.

Whitey D'Arcy. Mostly you see Whitey after dark in the soft glitter of some joint on Sunset between La Cienega and Beverly Hills, but I've run across him with troopers in a box at the Rams' games, or in a steam bath after golf at one of the movie-crowd country clubs. In Vegas around New Year's, naturally, and it used to be at the Flamingo there and now it's the newer places. Whitey D'Arcy, and whatever name he was born to wasn't D'Arcy, and the town that taught him life was maybe Detroit or Cleveland. I knew Whitey D'Arcy fairly well.

Tall, slender guy. Real blond hair in a brush cut, pale eyes. I'd seen his record: arrested on suspicion of homicide, arrested several times in various cities for carrying a weapon, arrested for narcotics sales, a couple of minor convictions, and all of that stuff years back.

"Hello, Oxford. Trying to find you, boy." A low voice, pale eyes watching me.

"Why?"

"Our pigeon, that do-gooder with the stuff — where is he?"

"Black?"

"Names yet? And everybody always said you were smart."

"What about him?"

"Where is he?"

"How should I know?"

D'Arcy's face never changed expression, his pale eyes never looked away.

"Oxford, you know what this is all about. What happened to you I don't know. But you loused this one bad. Orders are to stop the do-gooder and stop him here, not in L.A. We can't find him. I think you know."

There was no physical threat here. Whitey D'Arcy was not an idiot. We both knew what it was about. If I gave him trouble I'd pay for it, hard, but not here and not now. Likely I'd get my kidneys broken; it was the number-one big payoff for trouble guys. Mostly because it's such a permanent punishment, with the trouble guy remembering about it every pain-whipped night for the rest of his years-shorter life. If they didn't get me before I got to Big Q, they had friends in Quentin who'd smash my kidneys there. All accounts are paid off.

Some kids walked by us and D'Arcy moved aside courteously. He'd been practicing his manners for some years.

"I saw the man a few hours ago. I don't know where he is now."

"You working with him, Oxford?"

"No."

"Just between us boys, what went sour with you?"

Whitey D'Arcy would never understand why I had changed, never if I worked the rest of my life trying to explain. But I like my kidneys to stay in good shape and I had to keep straight with this man if I didn't want to spend the next few years bent over slightly to ease the pain.

"I loused it up. The guy doesn't scare or back away, and he got the idea the big men were going to try to stop him, so he got hot for this telecast tonight."

"He won't make it."

"That's what I told him."

"Why did you tell him that?"

I shrugged my shoulders. For years I've been keeping away from contacts with men like D'Arcy. Fight them and you don't fight one man or twenty men, you fight shadows until the organization that lives by terror kills or cripples you. Be around them and they'll make money from you, they'll take your women, and sooner or later they'll work you over, for laughs. Lots of men and women in Southern California know this by highly personal experience. Broken men and women.

Then I asked the wrong question. "You here with Mooney?"

The pale eyes never wavered. "I don't know the name."

D'Arcy is the principal owner of a big car dealership in Hollywood, he owns a chunk of apartment houses, he has a share in oil properties. All this is open knowledge, but the people of my world knew also that his title deeds were good only as long as he had power in the organization. If he lost the power they'd take his money, his women, and work him over, for laughs.

In the end, after all the money, the deals, the pretenses, the angles, the sharp talk, his power was based on terror.

I felt a little of that terror now, looking into the pale eyes. Roger Mooney was here, Whitey D'Arcy was here, the big machine was rolling to smash Ringling Black fast and completely. Because of Podden and me there was no time now for subtle tactics. This would be quick and brutal.

"You got any ideas that would help us, Oxford?"

"No."

"You going to keep your own nose clean from here on?"

"Yes."

"I hear around that you're in a bad jam. That right?"

"That's what I hear, too."

"Don't make it any harder on yourself, Oxford."

I didn't say anything. He walked toward the door above the outside steps. Through the open door the cool wind that comes from the ocean for an hour in the evening was suddenly chill.

"Tell you what you do, Oxford. This is a nice place. You just stay here. Right here. That's what I'm telling you to do—stay here."

Whitey D'Arcy walked out into the night. He'd found me easily enough and he had ways to keep on finding me.

Men being what they are, I went back to the telephone. I needed the woman. What she had for me was all that I had in the whole damn world. Let me be with her and the hell with all the rest of it.

This time the first ring broke off sharply and I heard her soft, husky voice.

"Yes?"

"Oxford. Hello, Nile."

"Where are you?" There was a taut insistence to her voice.

"Christian's."

"Stay there. I'll be right there."

I stood by the phone after she'd hung up, and then I put the receiver in its cradle. What I had wanted was to go to the big house over the entrance to the bay, close the front door, and forget the world. Instead I went to the bar.

She was there before I finished my drink. I stood up to give her my seat but she shook her head. She waited for me to come over to her, in the same spot where D'Arcy and I had talked. Some people in the bar knew her and waved. She smiled back at them, a small, pretty woman with a charm you could feel as if it were electric.

"Outside in my car." There was the same taut insistence.

We walked into the breeze-whipped darkness, around the pilings, the net, and the banana trees in front of the Hut, to the parking lot. She had her own car again, and it was empty. We got in, Nile behind the wheel.

"What is it, Nile?"

Her words sounded as if they were made of glass, brittle, ready to shatter. "Why did you call me?"

"I wanted to be with you, Nile. Maybe it isn't love, but it's something pretty powerful to me."

She turned her head and looked at me silently for many seconds.

"You must be insane."

"There's something going on here that I don't understand, Nile."

"Ringling Black was shot in his office about half an hour ago. He's at the Santa Ana hospital by now, and I was going there when you called."

I wasn't really surprised. One of D'Arcy's troopers putting tough pressure on Black, Black fighting, and that would be the way it could happen. I had felt that I was talking to a dead man when I had left him hours earlier.

"How bad?"

"I don't know yet. He was still alive."

"Why did you come here to see me?"

Again she looked at me, apparently in amazement. "It was your girl that shot him. The girl you were trying to use to frame him."

"Ann Field?"

"Ring told me about her. I think that's the name. It was the same girl. His secretary met her on the stairs as she went out for something. When she came back to close up she found Ring. He was almost conscious and he was trying to say something about the girl getting the evidence from him. She called the police and they called me — officially." Her voice was still soft, but it was lifeless.

"It couldn't have been Ann."

"It was."

"There was a hood — Whitey D'Arcy — here a few minutes ago. They were looking for Black and couldn't find him."

She answered in the same lifeless tone. "His secretary was alone in the office all afternoon. She told the police that several strangers had come by, and that there had been a lot of phone calls. Ring had showed up about five, and she went downstairs to the drugstore, meeting this girl coming up. When she came back Ring was on the floor. That was about ten minutes later."

I said again, "It couldn't have been Ann."

"After you left, Ring and I went for a long drive in his car. He took me downtown. I bought some things and took a cab home. My car was there. I don't know where King is. The phone was ringing when I opened the door, but the line was dead when I answered. A minute or so later the police called me. Then you called, as I was about to go to Santa Ana."

"Why did you come here, Nile?"

She seemed almost in pain, her mouth twisted, her eyes closed.

"I had to see you. Do you understand, Bill?"

It seemed incredible, but that was what she meant. Her arms were around me, her face against mine. After a minute she leaned away from me.

"Maybe this is hate, Bill. I don't know what it is, and don't trust me, Bill. Don't trust me."

My world was gone, lost in the whirlpool. I pulled her to me. This was in the parking area of Christian's Hut, in light-streaked darkness, and people walked only a few feet from the car. But that was the way it had to be. The whirlpool became the typhoon.

She was like a different woman now. There had been minutes of quiet and then she shook her head, rubbed her eyes.

"I told you not to trust me, Bill." She spoke normally now.

The strain was gone from me, too. I looked at her, her face almost hidden in shadow. If she bound me to her with soft chains, they must be steel-hard to her. My world came back to me and I did not welcome it.

"What about the stuff Black was to use on the

telecast?"

"It was in a flat leather envelope. The police say the secretary reports it gone. Ann took it."

It was strange, to talk this way after the violence we had just shared.

"I don't believe it."

"People in the nearby shops heard the shot. They didn't know where it came from. One man remembers seeing a girl — this Ann Field from the description — carrying a small leather envelope."

"You got all this from the police?"

"They read me the preliminary report and it only took a couple of minutes. You remember that I'm an assistant district attorney, Bill?"

"Naturally."

"Then you understand that I can do this. I'm arresting you for complicity in the shooting of Ringling Black. I'm sorry."

"You're crazy."

"Because of what just happened? Do you remember this noontime, Bill? Was it different for me than it was for you?"

"You can't believe that I'd be mixed up with shooting this man!"

"I can believe anything of a man, Bill. And a man can believe anything of me."

A car swung into the parking lot and its headlights made an edge of brightness for Nile's face. I felt a moral shock, a shaking of my whole structure of understanding people, such as I had not suffered since I was a boy.

"We've been together three times, Bill. Three times in less than one brief day. Once it was with a camera hidden outside the window and making pictures of us. Once it was violent, and I scratched and fought you. Once it was in love, or maybe hate, before I did what I must do to you. Did you want this thing of ours to be so terrible?"

I watched her, and the headlights blinked out. It was almost dark again.

"I'm glad it's been a terrible and violent thing, Bill. Glad — can you understand?"

"There isn't going to be an arrest, Nile."

Her hands touched my face. "Among savages it is the women who are most cruel, the women who torture. Women are still savage, Bill. You'll be taken anyway, the police will learn about Ann and you, but there's something strange and satisfying to me in arresting the man I love — or maybe hate."

"What about the telecast?" I couldn't share her sadistic-masochistic rites of emotion. It seemed that she felt close to me, closer than she had been to any man since John Lisbon. I felt no closeness to her now. My mind was with Ann somewhere in the night, under her arm a leather envelope worth the price of fifty million profit to the big men; with Ringling Black in emergency surgery at Santa Ana, with myself, trapped, defeated.

"There won't be any telecast. The evidence is gone. Ring may be dying. He couldn't believe that this is a brutal world, but we know, we know, Bill."

"I've got to find Ann."

"The police will find her. They'll roadblock the intersection at the end of Newport Beach and there's no other way out. She's trapped unless she got out right away. Bill, you're under arrest. You're my prisoner."

She turned on the ignition and I hit her under the

ear with the heel of my right hand, knocking her across the wheel and against the left front door. She moaned and I pulled her toward me with my left hand and hit her on the edge of her chin, solidly and carefully. Her head snapped and fell back. I had maybe a minute before she would start screaming.

I got out of the car, closed the door, and walked out the far end of the lot. The parking attendant stood there, and he waved to me. I waved back.

Maybe only thirty seconds more before she would come out of it and then she might scream. I hurried along the narrow street to the corner, turned, and ran toward the center of town. The clattering dissonance of some combo on a record was loud from a big house on the corner, its front door wide open. I could hear the laughter of kids.

I had to find Ann. Maybe if I could find her somehow I wouldn't be trapped or defeated. I wanted to fight back, and I needed Ann and the leather envelope to fight.

As Nile had said, "He couldn't believe that this is a brutal world, but we know, we know, Bill." Well, she knew.

CHAPTER THIRTEEN

Only as I reached the blare of noise and lights at Bay and Central did I realize how little chance there was of finding Ann. The police would be prowling through the crowds of kids, and they had started minutes ago to look for her. During Easter week the Newport Beach police added a dozen or so part-time officers to their regular staff of eight or ten. They had plenty of manpower to use in searching the two-mile-long, three-block-wide peninsula.

There were two ways out of Balboa and Newport — one by way of the chugging ferry to Balboa Island in the bay, and then over a short causeway to U.S. 101, the great coast highway leading north to Los Angeles and south to San Diego; the other way was down Central Avenue to its intersection with the same highway at a big concrete clover leaf under the bluffs that fringe the north end of Newport Beach.

Two roadblocks can seal off Newport and Balboa completely. It would be a poor town for a bank robbery.

I wondered if Nile had screamed. Proud, lovely woman in hell, and when you are with her you must share her hell. She had come to me because she needed me, and yet she had come also as the assistant district attorney of Orange County. Love or hate? With a man Nile Lisbon seemed to find little difference between them.

Ann Field. Where would she be, if they had not yet found her? She had talked with Podden, and then she had gone, hours later, to Ringling Black's office. Minutes after that he had been found shot, with the leather envelope gone. The evidence on the candidate in that envelope had been worth five thousand dollars to me this morning. What had Ann and Podden talked about? What did he offer her?

Ann Field. I tried to think as I walked. She had the envelope — where would she go? Podden was in jail as a vagrant, and I was sure that Mooney had started the machinery that put him there. Would she go to Mooney? He wouldn't let her come within fifty feet of him, even without the shooting. Mooney kept his hands very clean. Maybe Whitey D'Arcy. D'Arcy hadn't known about the shooting.

I was fighting. Trying to find Ann by myself was my declaration of war on the whole combination, the police, Mooney, D'Arcy, Nile. If I found her I might win part of a battle; maybe I'd know what happened in Ringling Black's office. With the leather envelope I'd have a weapon to fight with — a weapon that might cost the big men behind Mooney and D'Arcy fifty million and more. But what could I do with the weapon? How could I use it?

Bay Avenue was a carnival. Most of the kids were still in swimsuits, the younger ones clustered in the malt shops and hamburger-juke spots, the older ones drinking beer in the bars.

Down toward the Inn the crowd was thick along the sidewalk. My stuff was still in my room at the Inn, and my car was in the big ocean-front lot. The chances were against me on both of them if warrants had been out on me this afternoon. And if Nile Lisbon had set her dogs on me I was trapped in Balboa.

There was a tall girl in Easter-week uniform — a long sweater that reached to the bottom of brief shorts leaving her legs bare almost from the hips. A tall girl who was Ann Field wearing the one outfit that could hide her among the thousands of other girls on the sidewalks of Balboa tonight. In these lights she would look no older than the girls from U.C.L.A. and U.S.C. She was twenty feet away, walking on the side opposite the Inn.

I tried to run through the crowd and I bumped a lad of eighteen or so. He was with a group of three others, all of them dressed for the dance at the Rendezvous.

"Who you pushing, guy?" He grabbed me by the arm.

The special madness of the nine days for young

males comes at night, the time of the street fights in Balboa. The young men go back ten thousand years when the sun goes down. Laughing, friendly kids during the day, they become sullen, aggressive young bulls at night, quick to fight, restless, anxious to prove themselves.

I pulled his arm off.

"You're kind of clumsy, ain't you, pops?" he said. I was ten years or so older, far into middle age, and his natural enemy during these nine days. "Come down here looking for girls, did you, pops?"

The other three boys with him stood around us watching. Nobody else seemed to notice.

"Yah, every time Kirk puts on a coat with padded shoulders he thinks he's got to fight somebody," one of the kids said to another, laughing.

"Why don't you get out of town, pops?" said the boy, and he swung on me.

I stepped away and one of the others got between us. I tried to see Ann and turned my head. A second boy of the crowd started to talk to me.

"You didn't want any trouble, did you, mister? Of course not. Kirk just gets excited, that's all." As he spoke, the fourth one stepped behind me and locked my arms in a simple judo. The second kid laughed.

"Mister, you're kind of simple, did you know that?"

"Hustle him down to the alley and we'll work him over," said Kirk, his voice tight and breathless. "We'll teach the old bastard to come down here. He's probably a queer."

I broke the judo with an elbow-fall-back, and the kid grunted as the elbow bruised his ribs. Kirk took a short jab over the heart and he doubled over. The next one put him straight against the building wall and his face was white, his mouth hanging open as he tried to get air. The other two boys stepped back, their hands down, looking surprised and uncertain. I walked away from them and they went to Kirk, who needed a little help. There was no more trouble.

I crossed the narrow street, running along next to the parked cars. Ann had turned and was walking back. She saw me and hurried to me.

"Ann! What happened?" I said in a quick whisper.

"I've been looking for you, waiting for you, Bill." She was carrying a small purse. I didn't see any leather envelope.

"The police are hunting for you, Ann! Let's walk out on the pier — fast."

We walked through the crowds, past Kirk and his three friends at the end of the street. The four boys looked away, talking nervously among themselves. Ann and I went out across the beach to the long Balboa pier. Other couples were spaced along the walkway that stretched over the phosphorescent waves breaking into spray.

"What happened, Ann?"

"Are you O.K., Bill?" Her hands were tight on my forearm.

"Sort of. Tell me the story. Did you shoot Black?"

"I've got the envelope, Bill. You'll be all right." She was speaking in an excited breathlessness.

"Did you shoot Ringling Black?"

"Shoot him? No, of course not. I took the envelope, I've got it hidden."

"Better tell me the whole story, Ann."

"Why, you know it, Bill. You know what I did."

"All I know is that you planned to take a bus home, Ann. Then I saw you with Harry Podden. A few minutes ago I was told that Ringling Black was shot this evening and the police think you shot him. I don't know much else."

"Harry Podden was waiting for me when I checked out of that motel. He said he was a friend of yours. Isn't he?"

"No."

"But he knew my name, where I'd been staying, almost everything — "

"He's a private detective. He shadowed me yesterday."

"Oh." The girl seemed to slump, and her face was turned away from me. "Why am I always fooled? I can't learn can I? But why do they always lie to me?"

I put my arm around her. "It will be all right, Ann. Tell me the rest."

"Podden said that you were in deep trouble — facing prison. He said the only way you could square yourself was to get the evidence against a candidate that Ringling Black had. He said there wasn't much time."

"What did he want you to do?"

"At first he didn't say. He tried to find out how I felt about you. I'd only left you a little while before — and I guess I'm kind of foolish, Bill. I know that I never meant anything to you, but I told you that once I was crazy in love with you. I've hated you a lot since then, hated you so that I could kill you. But that little time yesterday, it was like seeing a new world. I was all back in love with you again, no matter how you felt about me. Excited and happy. Then Podden told me you were going to prison and only that evidence of Black's could be traded to get you out of trouble."

She was near to sobbing, and she was trying to be brave.

"Then after he found out how I felt he said I could help. He said that he would use force to get the stuff from Black's office except that he had a family and you wouldn't let him take the risk. He told me I was the only person who could help you. Mr. Black had talked to me when I went to him this morning and he told me what he was going to do about that candidate. He showed me the leather envelope and said he'd make arrangements to show the evidence on TV."

We must have looked much like other lovers of the nine days of spring as we stood in the darkness on the pier, a slim, long-legged girl with a man whose arm was around her, who looked into her face as she talked.

"Podden gave me a gun. The way I felt after we'd talked, you know, about me working in a store, and you selling for somebody, and having dates for swimming and movies — I'd been kind of dreaming all the way back to the motel. They were crazy dreams, but they were the best dreams I've had in a long time, Bill. I took the gun."

She pulled away from my arm, looked out toward the blackness of sea and sky.

"For a while I had a friend — oh hell, I lived with one of Whitey D'Arcy's guys for six months. Happy Murphy, just a guy. He was a collector for a Wilshire Boulevard bookie office. They called him Happy because he was gun-happy, always fooling around with them. He never shot anybody, he was strictly with the roll of nickels; you know, break the fellow's jaw with them if the fellow owed the book some money too long. Anyway, I know about guns from Happy."

Her voice sounded like lead slugs falling on a piece of stone.

"Podden told me to go to the office late. Mr. Black's secretary had told him over the phone that Mr. Black would be in late before driving up to Los Angeles. Podden said that Black would rather hand over the envelope than take a chance on being shot by a crazy girl with a gun. Podden would be in his car on Bay and I'd just toss the envelope in the window and keep going. He said it would save you from prison."

She turned back to face me. Bitterly she said, "It sounded like a frantic kick to me, but I thought the guy was your friend. He talked desperate and he looked real worried. Hell, I'd have cut off my leg with a dull knife for you after those few minutes there on the street. Yeah, I took the gun."

I waited and we both were silent.

After half a minute she began again. "I got my stuff out of the motel and checked it. I walked around and figured how to do this thing. In a store on Central I bought a swimsuit for fourteen bucks and I had the sweater. In the ladies' room of a beer joint on Bay I changed into the swimsuit. I wore a skirt, coat, and the sweater over it.

"I figured I'd try my play with Black and duck out. If I had the envelope I'd throw it in Podden's car and head for the parking lot, where I could slip out of my coat and skirt. In this town there are a jillion girls in sweaters and swimsuits. Podden said that once he had the envelope, the big wheels in L.A. would square any rap for me, and they'd let you get off the hook.

"For a couple of hours I fooled around, talked to some kids, stuff like that. Then I waited for Black to show. I saw him go up to his office and then I saw his secretary come out, so I went up."

"You passed her on the stairs?"

"Why, no. She was on the sidewalk before I even crossed the street."

"I think she says she passed you on the stairs."

"She did — when I was coming down. I might have looked funny because I was in a hell of a hurry. I had the envelope under my coat and I took it out when I got to where Podden was supposed to be, but he wasn't there."

"What happened in Black's office?"

"I walked in, with the gun out. Not nervous or anything, real dead cool. He gave a kind of yelp and started talking slow and easy, moving toward me. I took a pretty good aim down low and I talked cold and short. He caught on and stopped moving. Then I told him to give me the envelope — put it on a chair and back away. He put up a big argument and I was getting hot on the time. About then he looked scared and did like I told him. I took the envelope and backed out. He came charging through the door a moment later and found me standing there with that gun high, waiting. He slowed down fast and I made him go into the closet and I slipped a chair under the knob. I was feeling high and clear, like you do on gage.

"On the stairs I passed his secretary and I think she could hear him pounding on the door."

"What did you do with the gun?"

"Lord! That's the one thing I forgot all about! After I wedged the chair I must have left it on the girl's desk while I put the leather envelope under my coat. I forgot it completely!"

"You didn't shoot him?"

"No. But I know he was shot. They were talking about it on the street."

"Didn't that surprise you, Ann?"

"I got scared. No Podden. After I got out of there and there wasn't any Podden, I went to the parking lot and stripped down to my suit and sweater. Then I walked along the ocean toward Newport. I could hear a lot of sirens. Maybe then or twenty minutes later I came back. My clothes and the envelope are inside the gate of a closed-up house on Ocean Front. I kind of mixed with the crowds around the Inn, figuring you might come there. Some of the people were talking about Ringling Black's being shot and there was a prowl car at the corner where his office is. I got real scared — but I didn't shoot him. All the while I was thinking about things and I never thought about the gun. That's strange, isn't it?"

"What were you going to do, Ann?"

"I was mixed up. If I didn't find you, well — "

"Yes, Ann?"

Her face was upturned toward mine, her eyes almost luminous in the light from the pier lamps.

"What could I do, Bill? They'd watch the buses and cars. I couldn't put my clothes on. I guess I figured that if I couldn't find you, well, I sort of would let myself get picked up for a party somewhere. What else could I do, Bill? After a while I'd have to get off the streets and there was no place for me to stay and I couldn't get away. What else could I do, Bill?"

She had a good question there. I knew another one: What could the two of us do now?

I had a private question. In the last few years Ann Field had done a lot of lying to men. They lied to her, and she lied to them. How much of her story to me was a lie?

CHAPTER FOURTEEN

"You would do all that for me? Risk an armed holdup of a lawyer in his own office, Ann?"

"Why not? I've been trying to change my way of living for a long time. It's never worked out. Today I thought this time there might be a chance, because of you. When Podden told me it was either the stuff that Black had or you in jail — "

She talked like the sin-scarred girl these last years had made her, her voice flat with an edge of bitterness. But I could remember how she had been earlier.

"Now what, Bill? Did I louse things up again?"

"We're going to have to try to get out of town. Maybe in Los Angeles I can fix things."

"Bill Oxford — the fixer." She said it and laughed a little.

"This is one I'll have to fix. This is the big one and the last one, Ann."

"Still feel the same way?" Ann was close, her words almost a whisper.

"Yes."

"But when you're tired of getting up at six in the morning, and wearing cheap clothes, and eating in hash houses, then what? And maybe if you should meet some nice kid and get married, you know, somebody you could love, wouldn't you want to get her fine stuff, and a big house, and then there might be kids — "

"There weren't any nice girls for the old Bill Oxford, and he wouldn't have made much of a father, Ann. Worried, excited, drunk, getting cheaper at a higher price all the time. I won't go back to it and I can't go back. I'll take the hash houses and all the rest and be damn happy. If I can."

We both were silent, looking out toward the darkness over the great, murmuring Pacific.

"Let's get your clothes and the envelope. That's our only ace now, Ann."

"About three blocks down along Ocean Front, behind the gate of a closed-up house."

"Let's go," I said, and we walked back on the pier toward the jingle of Balboa.

"I didn't shoot him, Bill. He was in the closet, pounding on the door. Believe me, Bill." Ann was holding my arm, her slim body close to mine.

"Somebody sure did, and the cops have your name as the last person with him. Your name and the gun Podden gave you, which maybe can be traced through him to you. If Black dies — "

I could feel the shudder in her body.

"You might as well know it, Ann. I'm in this jam just as hot as you are. About twenty minutes ago I slugged a district attorney who was arresting me on suspicion of a plot between you and me to rob and shoot Ringling Black."

"You slugged a district attorney?"

"An assistant, a woman. I know her. She was a — a friend."

"A friend? And she was putting the collar on you?"

"She's sort of a strange woman. Maybe I understand her, maybe I don't."

"Do you like her?"

That was a tricky word to use for what I felt for Nile Lisbon. I didn't like her. She picked up strange men the way a wolf picks up girls. She had two, maybe more men who loved her or thought they did, and she cheated openly and boldly on them. She lived three lives — the socially prominent young career woman; the mistress of King McCarthy, the rough, swaggering driver of a cannery semitrailer; the seeker after a man who could fully replace a dead man. I didn't like her very much. Love? The whirlpool, the typhoon, the electric charm? That was something else again.

"In a way, I'm crazy about her," I said.

We were walking along Ocean Front, which is merely a sidewalk along the two miles of sandy Pacific beach, lined with small and big houses that are mostly vacant until the summer season. A few of the Easter-week kids were strolling here, but not many.

"She knew my name?" Ann was walking at my side, but her body was no longer touching mine.

"Ringling Black told her. They've been friends for a long time."

"A town like this one," said Ann, "everybody knows everybody else, until the summer crowds, of course. Did you know this lady district attorney before?"

"I met her last night. Yesterday afternoon in a Newport bar, actually. We got to a point where we were both talking about love this morning."

"One of those things." Ann's voice was flat again. "You and she talk about love and she tries to put you in the jug. I stick up a lawyer for you. Well, that's the way it goes and always will go."

We were beyond the casual strollers now and Ocean Front was a yellow line of street lamps stretching toward Newport and an empty, breeze-swept sidewalk in the night. Ann was watching the houses and she stopped in front of one near a street lamp. She pushed open the gate and we stepped into a winter-dead garden behind a low wall. Next to the wall was a bundle. Ann picked it up and handed me the leather envelope. Then, standing straight and facing me, she slipped off her sweater and her one-piece swimsuit. The street light painted her skin with gold.

"A lot of different guys have seen me like this, but somehow you never have, have you, Bill?"

She was slim, and whatever the years had done to her, they had not touched her body.

I stood there and she waited for a moment, and then silently she got into her skirt, sweater, and coat. She let the swimsuit lie where it had fallen in the winter-dead garden.

"The stuff I should be wearing under this is checked in a locker at the pavilion. Can we risk getting them?" Ann was brushing her skirt with her hands.

"No. Balboa is more than just hot for both of us now — it's probably burning up."

"Well, technically, I won't be a nice girl, if you understand what I mean."

"We've got to find a phone booth somewhere, Ann. I'm going to start fixing."

We walked along the beach silently. It was about seven o'clock, and Ringling Black's television time was at nine. I was holding the power in my hand, the power of truth about a corrupt and venal candidate, but by tomorrow the powerful forces behind him would have had their chance to work and probably the stuff in the leather envelope would be destroyed or worthless.

Four short blocks along Ocean Front was a hamburger and malt store with a phone booth outside. I had plenty of change. First I called the program manager of the Rockwood network's Los Angeles station, identifying myself as an associate of Ringling Black.

"You've heard about Mr. Black?" I asked him.

He sounded careful and reserved. "No. We've had quite a bit of pressure put on us over this political telecast tonight, however. You may tell Mr. Black that we are placing our confidence in his legal judgment as to the matters he intends to discuss tonight and we will carry the program as scheduled."

"Mr. Black has been injured in an accident. He is now at the Santa Ana Community Hospital."

"Oh!" I could almost hear his program-managing mind spinning into gear. "Mr. Black is familiar with television appearances and we've made some unusual allowances in scheduling this sudden change for this political telecast because of our respect for his ability — and, if you'll forgive the word, his talent."

"We're sending an experienced replacement. He should reach the studio by eight-thirty or so. Hold the program exactly as scheduled."

"We've got Mr. Black timed for two cameras in Studio D, with the switch to Mr. Black — or his replacement — at nine-five."

"O.K. Studio D, as scheduled."

"Thank you. I hope Mr. Black — "

I hung up. Time was a fire burning at the slim packet of power that I held in a leather envelope. I called the Santa Ana Hospital.

"Is Mrs. Lisbon there? She may be with an emergency patient, Ringling Black."

"Mrs. Nile Lisbon? Yes, I saw her a moment ago. I'll get her for you. Who is calling, please?"

"Oxford. Bill Oxford." Why try to be clever? I held the receiver for nearly half a minute before I heard her voice.

"Hello, Bill." This was the woman who had come to me in passion only an hour ago, and the last time I had seen her she was unconscious because I had slugged her. The words were very low, soft. "You hit awfully hard."

"Listen carefully, Nile. I want to make a bargain."

"I'm a poor bargainer, Bill. Not a good law officer either, I'm afraid. But I had to do what I did all of what I did — and you had to do what you did. You may not be much else, Bill, but you're a man."

Empty words. "Time is damn tight, Nile. I'll make Ringling Black's telecast for him tonight. I've got the stuff and that's what counts, regardless of how clumsy I might be in front of the camera. I've been around scores of shows in rehearsal and productions."

"So?"

"That's part of my bargain. The rest of it is that I'm with Ann Field. I'll turn her over to you."

"What? Are you double-crossing somebody else now? Women can't trust you much, can they?" Strange woman; she sounded amused.

"Your part of the bargain is to get me to the studio in Los Angeles by eight-thirty. Being in your car is probably the only way I can get out of Newport."

"Why should I bargain, Bill? The Field girl can't get out of Newport either. We'll get her without your help, maybe in the next hour or so. As far as making the telecast — if you really intend to — that doesn't mean much to me, though it might to Ring."

"How is he?"

"Not too bad. They took out the bullet and put him under morphine."

"Making that telecast is important to me, Nile. Damn

important. If I make it I'll be a dead pigeon. I know that. But the guys who will cook me for it will know that Bill Oxford is straighter and tougher than they ever thought he was. And I'll know it, too."

She was silent for a moment. Then, soft and husky, "I understand, Bill. What do you want me to do?"

"Drive to Newport. That will take about twenty minutes or less. Meet us at Nineteenth and Ocean Front, at the dead end where Nineteenth comes up to the beach."

"I'll be there in twenty minutes or less, Bill. Does the Field girl know you're going to turn her in?"

"Not yet."

"I'll see you, Bill."

I hung up and pushed the phone-booth door open. Ann was standing on the walk, her head high, the sea breeze riffling her hair, looking toward the lights of a ship miles out in the black Pacific.

CHAPTER FIFTEEN

The fixer. Using people, lying a little here, hiding something there, with a telephone as a tool. Bill Oxford, the fixer, trying to fix the big one, and the last one. I had to save Ann and myself, but it was going to be tricky.

She turned to look at me, waiting for me to speak.

"Nile Lisbon is coming to meet us, Ann."

"Isn't she the one you slugged a little while ago?"

"That's right."

"And she's coming to meet you. It's certainly the damnedest love affair I've ever heard about, and I've heard some doozies. What are you going to do this time — beat her brains out with a bat? Or is she bringing a sheriff's posse to shoot you down?" Ann finished with the little empty laugh she had learned in the last few years.

"I've made a deal with her. I'm going to try to do Black's telecast at nine: she's going to drive me there."

Ann guessed. Her body stiffened and her arms hung at her sides. "What's your part of the bargain, boy?"

"You."

She slapped me across the face and my aching jaw almost burst with pain. I stood there. "Always, always, always!" she sobbed. "Why? Why do I always get used, lied to, cheated? Every damn time, every damn time!"

She turned away, sobbing. I put my arms around her. She tried to break away from me but I held her gently.

"I'm going to get you out of this, clean and clear, Ann." I had to say it over and over, slowly, before the words cut through the hate and bitterness that stormed in her mind. The hysteria quieted into spasms of crying.

"We were trapped, both of us. They would have found us and that would have been the end. If the police got us into cells tonight, neither of us would know anything but a cell for the next five years. Do you understand, Ann? We were trapped, trapped right down the line. I couldn't figure from a cell."

"So you're out and I'm in," she said brokenly. "That's fine, fixer."

"Nobody's in. I'm not done fixing, Ann, I've only started."

She wiped her face with a handkerchief from her small purse.

"What do you mean?"

"To start with, Ann, I believe your story about meeting Black's secretary on the way out, instead of on your way in, as she tells it. That's a hell of a big difference, and I believe you. I believe you didn't shoot him. He's under morphine now and he can't talk, but if he recovers he'll tell who did the shooting."

"It wasn't me."

"Whitey D'Arcy's in town. It was either one of his men — or Black's secretary."

"Why would she shoot her boss?"

"Who knows? It's happened before. But you did go in there with a gun, and you did take the leather envelope at gunpoint."

"Yes."

"That's armed robbery, Ann, regardless of why you did it. That's one of the things I've got to fix. I'm playing it the best way I know how."

"By turning me in to your girl friend so that she looks great?"

"Your other choice is getting picked up by some Newport cop. If Black recovers you'd be charged with armed robbery; if he doesn't it would be murder in the first. That's a tough one."

"And what's different this way?"

"You'll see."

"Bill, are you playing it straight with me? For God's sake, don't lie, don't lie this one time!"

"I'm playing it straight."

She was looking at me, trying to see my face in the light of the street lamp across the way.

"O.K., Bill."

We both let it go at that for a quiet moment. The only sound was the beat of the sea on the sand and the night wind.

I could almost feel the minutes grinding by on the face of my watch. After seven now, and Studio D would be waiting with two cameras at exactly nine-five. Until that moment I was still the man with the power.

If I missed the telecast I could try crawling back to Roger Mooney, give him the leather envelope, claim that I had done the job I'd been sent to Balboa to do — stop Ringling Black. Maybe I'd get my five thousand, I might even try to put a fix in for Ann Field. I could twist things around, lie fast and often, and maybe come out of it with my dirty reputation a little dirtier, and still worth dirty money.

It might even be easy to get myself out of the jam right now. Five thousand — and maybe I could stick them for ten. Pay off the debts, get the warrants canceled. Mooney respected one thing, success, and if I was the one who had the leather envelope, I could get my job back in the agency, and the lunches at Lucey's, Romanoff's, and the Beverly Hills Country Club would continue. Just one more double cross in six years of crosses and I wouldn't have a worry in the world. No hash-house meals, no cheap clothes — nothing but the best for Bill Oxford, the fixer.

"I've got a couple of phone calls to make, Ann," I said. "Just keep waiting here."

My first try with the telephone hit the right place. Mooney was in the bar at the Balboa Inn, chief spider in the web, waiting for reports from all the little spiders.

"Mooney?"

"Yes? Is that you Oxford?" He recognized my voice, and I could sense the tension in his. The big spider was worried.

"It's Oxford. I've got the leather envelope of Black's

with the photostats and the affidavits, the whole works."

"Good boy, Bill, good boy! I knew you were a little upset today, but I knew you'd come through. You always have. Where are you?"

"On my way to Los Angeles. You know Black was shot tonight?"

"Of course. If — well, if there's any question about being involved in that, maybe you'd better go up to San Francisco or somewhere and take a brief vacation. Don't call me, or call the agency, just keep that envelope safe. We'll see how things work out, and you'll be taken care of, we'll fix things. You know the agency can fix things."

"Yeah. Only I'm going to Los Angeles to see that the telecast is made, and that the punk crook candidate your crowd is backing couldn't be nominated for county midwife. Understand, Mooney? I'm going to play this one straight, and as you say, I always come through."

"Oxford! Don't be insane! The agency — "

I hung up on him. Then I called the private number of a man I knew on the Los Angeles *Daily News*.

"This is Bill Oxford," I said when I recognized his voice on the phone.

"Yes?" He was a hard-working, decent, and honest newspaperman, and I didn't rate too well with that kind.

"Your office will have a bulletin on the shooting of Ringling Black, prominent Orange County attorney late this afternoon. Here's the rest of the story."

"What's your interest in this, Oxford?" It was a cold, suspicious question.

"Naturally I've got an angle, Matt, but you can check out the facts I'll give you."

"O.K. What is it?"

"Black had arranged at noon today to do the regular political telecast on the primary at nine tonight. He had photostats and affidavits on the high-powered candidate that would blow the jerk out of the race. A lot of force was used to try to stop Black. This afternoon, around five, he was shot and wounded. I've got the evidence and I'm taking it to the station for that telecast."

"Whoa, Oxford. I don't get this. You've never worked with the clean crowd, you run with the other side. This doesn't sound kosher."

"Check the facts. It's the Rockwood network station. Do me a favor."

"That's what I was waiting for, Oxford."

"Don't mention or use my name until after the telecast. Check all you want to, but don't use my name."

"I won't and you're damn right I'll check. Thanks, Oxford."

He hung up. So that was that. It might be hash houses, and it might be the prison mess hall at San Quentin, but it wasn't going to be Romanoff's or the Beverly Hills Country Club.

I must have looked better to Ann when I came out of the phone booth. Maybe I carried myself straighter or something.

"Bill," she said coming close, "tell me about this woman district attorney."

"Nile Lisbon. You know about her husband, John Lisbon. She's a woman that has caught fire inside, somehow, and she's burning up herself and the men around her. She's a woman with a powerful, intangible physical charm. She's hunting for a complete man —

one that the fire won't destroy. She has to find him."

"What woman doesn't?" Ann asked, and seconds later said, "And how few ever find them."

"Most women give up. Nile doesn't. She's aflame from that fire within her and I'm afraid soon she'll destroy herself in it. She's got a lot, this charm, beauty, a career, social position, and the ability to fascinate. Not many women are like, her, but some regulator, some balance wheel, is missing. She's going faster, faster — "

"You say all this, Bill, and yet you think you love her?"

"It's not anything that words will explain, Ann. I met her yesterday and we've lived in violence together much of the time since yesterday. It seems as if there's something about each of us that generates violence around us when we're together. I had to fight the man she was with the first time I saw her, I fought him again and we almost killed each other, and now he's somewhere in this town looking for me, and he intends to kill me."

"Good Lord, Bill! Maybe I'm not much good for men, but — "

We both turned as the headlights of a car swept up along the dead-end street behind us. The lights outlined us like a stage spot.

The car stopped, turning to parallel the sidewalk of Ocean Front. It looked like Nile Lisbon's car.

"I think that's her," I said to Ann.

Her hand found mine, squeezed it.

"You're playing it straight, Bill." It wasn't a question.

"Straight and hard," I said.

The car door opened. Ann dropped my hand. She was standing, shoulders back and chin high, slim and lovely and brave.

"Hello, Bill!" Nile was by the side of her car.

From the other side of the car a man swung out, and in the yellowish light I saw King McCarthy, slipping off his leather jacket and walking toward me, feet wide apart, hands out and forward.

Nile said, clear and soft, "I've wanted to see this ever since yesterday. They would have stopped it yesterday, but nobody will stop it now."

King was moving slowly, and his teeth shone in the light, his mouth drawn back in his terrible smile.

Behind us were sand and the surf of the Pacific. There were two women to watch us, and only the yellow glow of the street lamp for light.

I had a funny thought as I waited for King to make his rush: This has been one hell of a day for my face.

The minutes and seconds were grinding away, and if I missed the telecast tonight there would be no second chance, no out, no anything.

King was five feet away, his teeth still shining.

Nile spoke, "I like getting hit by a man, Bill. But I've got to be sure he's a man. Against another man."

CHAPTER SIXTEEN

McCarthy rushed, head low, both forearms horizontal, fists only six inches or so apart. I'd break my hands quickly if I tried hitting him on his jaw, cheek, or forehead, so I took his rush like a wrestler, turning my body to the side as he charged in. The leather envelope was thrown on the sidewalk.

His left fist was shooting into a punch as I turned and I grabbed the wrist with my left hand, throwing my right shoulder into the side of his head. King stumbled and both of us moved from the sidewalk into the soft sand of the beach.

McCarthy, his left wrist still locked in my left hand, tried a high, wild right for my face. I crashed into him with my shoulder again and we rolled into the sand. He broke my hold and knocked me off him with a short, solid right that hammered my aching face. It was the punch that lost him the fight, but I didn't know that. His knuckles broke, splitting between the first and the second fingers of his right hand.

I went backward into the sand, shoulders flat, knees high. McCarthy was on his feet and he jumped for me, both heels aimed for my chest. As the boots came down I was twisting. One missed and one raked across my ribs, throwing him off balance. My hand pulled his right ankle sharply over as I kept rolling and he went down, my shoulder on his right shin, his left boot heel stabbing at my spine. While he kicked at me I tried to break his ankle but he pulled loose and scuttled backward across the sand like a crab.

We were both up, crouching at the same time, and I waited for his rush. He came in and his left fist opened at the end of a long, straight one, grabbing my hair. He tried to bring the heel of his right hand up under my chin, and I smashed him away from me with rights and lefts to the body, his fingers pulling hair as he went back. He charged in again and as we closed his right knee came up hard, and I fell back bringing my left knee up and catching his right leg between shin and kneecap. I could see his grinning teeth in front of me and then his head went back like a football at the end of a kick as my knee forced his right leg high against his body. As he went over I brought my left foot into him but missed the killing kick.

This time I tried the jump, my heels landing right on his midsection, but I fell to the side and scrambled clumsily in the deep sand. He didn't get up, but he wasn't through yet. I was breathing like a mile runner at the tape and I stayed back waiting. He got to his knees slowly and when I came forward he threw a handful of sand in my eyes. King grabbed my belt and pulled himself up with his head butting into my chin and snapping my skull back. His left fist went deep into my belly.

I brought my heels down on the soft leather over his instep as his arms went round me, lifting me from the sand and bearing me back toward the sidewalk. He intended to fall on me, smashing the back of my head into jam on the concrete. This man was trying to kill me. My first and second fingers stabbed into his eyes and we fell together on the sidewalk.

The rough cement ripped my ear. He tried for my throat with both hands, and his teeth were wide apart for a bite somewhere on my face or throat. My arm was around his head and I found his ear, pulling his head until I thought the ear would tear away. His teeth came down to the skin of my face and I slid my left hand under his nose, pushing his face away with the heel of my hand.

He pulled away and up into a crouch and I jerked my whole body on my shoulders, getting him with both my heels to his face. He went back, yelling, and I rolled over and up. His fingers were at his eyes, trying to wipe away the blood, and he got back to a kneeling position. This time my left foot caught him under the chin and his head missed the edge of the slab by a couple of inches or he would have died with a melon-split skull.

I used my foot to kick his right leg across the sharp slab edge and then I jumped on it, breaking the long shinbone. The fight was over.

Ann was at my side and I was shaking terribly, even my teeth were chattering. I didn't know where I was hurt or how badly.

King was trying to hold his broken leg with one hand while the other was over his crushed face, fingers spread apart as if he were trying to push the small bones together again. He was a used man.

Nile went to him, bent over, and tried to say something. He didn't listen. He pulled himself to the sidewalk slab that had knifed through his shin, and tried to get into a sitting position. Nile helped him.

With Ann's arm around me I limped toward Nile. Ann was carrying the envelope.

"Call doc f'him. Geh me station. No time," I mumbled through the swirl of pain that was my mouth and jaws. I could feel the wetness of my clothes now, wet through and clammy.

Now Nile stood and faced me, but first she and Ann measured each other in the pale yellow lamplight.

Then Nile spoke to me. "You almost killed him, didn't you? He would have killed you."

"Why did you bring that man? Who is he?" said Ann, angry and loud.

"King McCarthy. He thought he had a debt of honor to settle with Oxford. It's settled for a long time to come now, because I'm afraid he's been broken for good. Not dead — broken."

"You know who I am."

"You're the girl who shot Ringling Black in his office."

It was hard for me to talk. There didn't seem to be

any air in my lungs. I wondered if my jaw was broken, and all the other pains were blazing into fire now — hands, fingers, belly, feet, scalp. Another minute and he would have had me like a paper doll to tear apart.

"I didn't shoot Mr. Black. Bill Oxford knows that. You'd better call a doctor for that man. He's hurt bad."

Nile went to find a phone booth and Ann wiped at my face with a handkerchief, my scraped ear oozing quite a bit of blood that trickled over my cheek.

"Lord, I was scared," said Ann. "I had my slipper off but I didn't dare try with the heel because you both were all jumbled together. Do you think you're hurt bad, Bill?"

I shook my head, slowly, and even that hurt plenty. McCarthy was resting on one arm and trying not to moan. I hoped I hadn't ruptured his intestines with my heels. King McCarthy was rough. If that bartender yesterday had known how rough King was, he wouldn't have teased him with that sawed-off baseball bat. That's what I was thinking about now.

Nile came back to us. "The ambulance will be here in a few minutes. Do we wait?"

"I got geh station nine," I mumbled.

"All right, man. You made your deal and you won your fight. Miss Field, you'd better come with us. As an assistant district attorney of this county I'm arresting you on suspicion of the attack on Ringling Black."

Ann looked at me. I nodded.

"O.K.," said Ann. "I'm arrested. Now what?"

"We'll all go to Los Angeles. That's the deal I made. And we'll all come back. It's not quite legal, but it's the deal."

"What about this man? Are you going to leave him

here alone?" asked Ann.

"With the siren on my car and the red spotlight on, maybe we can make that station by ten minutes to nine. Do you want to leave now or wait, Bill?"

"Lea'," I said.

The three of us got into the front seat of Nile's car, I in the middle. Nile had said something into King's ear before she got into the car but he had not answered. He wanted to be alone, a rough fighter who had lost a rough fight.

By the time we were on Central we could hear the siren of the ambulance going toward the place where King McCarthy waited.

"What's your story on Ringling Black?" asked Nile as she drove, her red spot flashing along the highway and her siren wailing into the night.

"Should I tell her, Bill?"

"Yeah." I was massaging my face with my fingertips. We passed the clover-leaf intersection at the edge of Newport. Two local police cars were there, and I saw a sheriff's car on the other side. The officers were stopping all cars going north on 101 or out of Newport. Nile didn't even slow down, but she clicked on her two-way radio.

"This is Mrs. Lisbon of the district attorney's office. I am going to Los Angeles on an investigation. Out." She lit a cigarette for me and one for herself. "Go ahead, Miss Field."

Nile was doing seventy-five now, slowing to sixty when we passed through a business district. She was a cool, skillful, nerveless driver.

"A private detective named Harry Podden told me to go to Ringling Black's office to get certain papers in a leather envelope that I had already seen," said Ann, her words carefully chosen and stilted. "Mr. Podden gave me a revolver for my protection. Mr. Black and I got into a disagreement and I was forced to lock him in a closet for my own protection. He was uninjured and well when I left, and I passed his secretary on the stairs as I was leaving the office."

Ann Field was one smart girl. Ringling Black couldn't have coached her to tell her story better than that if he were her attorney.

"Say that last again," said Nile.

Ann repeated herself.

"I'll be damned," muttered Nile. "The funny thing is I believe you."

She spoke into the radiophone again. "This is Mrs. Lisbon. Please phone the Santa Ana Community Hospital and get a report on Ringling Black for me. And, oh, yes, phone them again in about ten minutes and get the emergency report on a King McCarthy. That's a street-fight case. Thank you. Out."

The phone burbled back at her. I didn't try to listen. Nile kept the car barreling through the night toward the Santa Ana freeway, direct road to Los Angeles.

"You know Betty Parker, the secretary, by sight?" asked Nile.

"I saw her this morning, in the reception room of Mr. Black's office. A small, neat girl."

"That's Betty Parker. Ring's partner, Jay Packard, has been at court in Santa Ana all day. And you saw Betty Parker going up the stairs as you were coming down, not the other way around?"

"No. Mr. Black was pounding on the closet door, I was going down, she was coming up. The small, neat girl. I recognized her but she didn't speak to me."

"You had the envelope then?"

"Yes."

"Miss Parker wasn't there when you came up?"

"No."

"I'll be damned," said Nile again.

I was beginning to feel better and worse. Better because I could breathe now, and the heat of my body was drying my sweat-soaked clothes. Worse because my ear hurt, and everything else in my body hurt.

The radiophone burbled. It was something about Black. Still under narcotics, but his condition was good.

Nile spoke into the phone. "Thank you. This is Mrs. Lisbon. Miss Elizabeth Parker, Ringling Black's secretary, was released after questioning this evening. Pick her up again and hold her at the Newport Beach police station for questioning by me when I return. Book her open. Out."

Nile was competent, confident. This was no woman afire now. I could understand, for the first time clearly, how the three levels of her life operated. This Nile Lisbon had the smooth assurance to carry her anywhere as a successful young career woman. The violently emotional and passion-whipped woman who had brought King McCarthy to fight me was hidden now beneath the cool surface of a woman who knew her job.

"What became of the gun this Podden gave you?" Nile asked, turning her head.

"I left it on the secretary's desk."

"In what condition?"

"Loaded and with the safety off," answered Ann coolly.

"I see. What was your relationship to this Harry Podden?"

"He asked me to get the leather envelope and its contents."

"You worked for him?"

"No."

"You were friends?"

"No. I met him today for the first time."

"Did he offer you money?"

"No."

"Did he force you with threats? Blackmail or threats of arrest?"

"No."

"Then why did you do it?"

Ann didn't answer. I said, speaking fairly clearly now although it still hurt, "Ann did it for personal reasons. Podden lied to her."

"I think I understand."

For minutes Nile tooled her car through the freeway traffic at speeds around seventy. The siren wailed, and at intervals there were bulletins on the radiophone.

"When we get near the station there may be some more trouble," I said.

"What kind?"

"Maybe gunmen. Whitey D'Arcy's men. The opposition knows an attempt will be made to do Black's expose on the political telecast at nine."

"Gunmen. What's the term — 'gunsels'? A shamus named Podden, and a ring of gunsels around the station. Melodrama, Oxford, melodrama!"

Ann's voice was cold. "I had a friend who used to read those books. A Jewish friend who found those words very funny. He explained to me that some writer named Dashiell Hammett used them first, years ago, and used them right, but since then other writers have picked them up without knowing what they really mean."

"Oh?" said Nile.

"A gunsel isn't a gunman. It's Yiddish for a young, weak homosexual. Shamus is a Yiddish word, too. It means somebody that's a know-it-all, not a private detective. A shamus is the janitor at a synagogue, and it's an old joke that he always acts as if he knows more than the rabbi. It's kind of funny."

"It's still melodrama, but thanks for the explanation," said Nile.

"You're always welcome," answered Ann. "You've asked me some questions. May I ask you a few?"

"Maybe. Try me."

"Why did you bring that man to fight Bill?"

"I'll answer that question to Bill himself, but you can listen. You're a woman, and I guess you know men. I don't. I'm a widow, a young widow, the kind they've made jokes about since the first young husband died, I suppose. My first experiment, when I started experimenting, was a fine, interesting man. But I'd lie awake through the night each time. There was nothing there for me. No male. Understand?"

"Certainly," said Ann. "Ever think it was maybe your fault too?"

"I thought about that a lot, Miss Field. But regardless of who was at fault, it wasn't any good with this fine, intelligent, successful, and all the rest of it man."

"So you experimented some more."

"Yes. Eventually I found King McCarthy, the man who was broken tonight. He was male. But he had nothing else much. He was a fighter, but he was afraid of me."

"Afraid of you?"

"Not in the ordinary way. Say he respected me — for my dead husband, for my job, for my friends. Maybe he was afraid I'd get tired of him, but he didn't think he could do anything about it. Maybe he even loved me. I didn't love him."

"Kind of selfish," said Ann.

Our car was wailing through the night, rolling away the forty miles to the studio. I listened, but I did not talk.

"Selfish, true," said Nile. "John — that was my husband, John Lisbon — said there were two kinds of women, the sock-washers and the non-sock-washers. The sock-washer is the kind who gets up before the man does and washes out his socks so they'll be clean and dry when he wakes. The non-sock-washer doesn't give a damn. I'm a sock-washer — but since John died I haven't found a man whose socks I'd wash. Do you understand what I mean? Of course, it has nothing to do really with socks."

"I understand."

"I don't know you, except that you're both my prisoners, but I get the idea you're fond of Bill Oxford. Bill and I have made love under some odd circumstances in the last twenty-four hours, damn odd circumstances."

"I see," said Ann, and she sounded far away and tired.

"Among other things Bill Oxford knocked me cold a couple of hours ago and it still hurts. King McCarthy found us together earlier today. They had a fight and Oxford knocked King out with a lamp. King hunted him all afternoon — to kill him."

"I don't want to hear this," Ann said.

"When you called me at the hospital, Bill, and offered

your deal, I hated you. I wanted to be clean of you, clean of the fixer, the schemer, the double-crosser. I hunted through the three places King might be and found him. I told him I'd bring him to you."

"He damn near killed me," I said.

"Do you blame him for trying?"

"No."

"I'd be a lot happier there in jail," said Ann. "At least I'd be alone."

"Right now all I care about is making that telecast," I said. "If I do that, maybe afterward I can look around and see who I am."

The radiophone burbled.

"Mrs. Lisbon ... Mrs. Lisbon ..."

"Here."

"Two reports, Mrs. Lisbon," said the impersonal voice. "King McCarthy suffered a broken leg, a broken nose and jaw, two broken ribs, bruises, and contusions. His condition is not critical.

"The other report is on Elizabeth Parker. En route to the station a few minutes ago she admitted shooting Ringling Black. She is giving a full statement now. She says she has been in love with Black and that he has been her lover. Late today he returned to the office and told her he was — was — "

"Told her he was going to marry me," Nile said softly.

The impersonal voice stammered and continued. "Parker's statement will be ready when you return. She admitted leaving the office and attempting to buy a quantity of sleeping pills with the intention of suicide. She was unable to purchase the pills and returned to the office. She found Black locked in a closet and there was a gun on her desk. She says she opened the door and shot him after learning that he had been robbed at gunpoint by a woman named Ann Field. Out."

"Thank you. Out."

Nile shook her head. "Poor girl. Poor Ring. I thought maybe there was something between him and Betty, but he swore there wasn't. Poor little kid."

She was silent. "I told you I loved you, Bill Oxford, and you didn't answer. Maybe I don't blame you. When you left this afternoon I felt whipped by the world. You. The pictures. What you did to me. The fight between you and King. Everything. My world was whipping me. I was tired and washed up. I told Ring that I'd marry him. That's why he got shot. He told Betty.

"And when I heard he was shot, you called, and I had to go to you. You know why."

She laughed, the empty, bitter little laugh like Ann's. "I'd thought I was a strong woman, in a little private hell of my own, but strong enough. Instead I've let my hell destroy Betty, and Ring, and McCarthy."

I didn't say anything, even though I knew she was waiting desperately for words.

CHAPTER SEVENTEEN

Nile was cutting through the heavier Friday night traffic of the industrial suburbs now, and whatever was storming in her heart and mind did not show in the way she handled the wheel.

Cars, trucks, and buses pulled toward the curb as their drivers saw the red spotlight and heard the scream of our siren. People on the sidewalks turned their heads and watched the sedan whip past them. I saw a blurred panorama of floodlighted supermarts, neon-embroidered bars, Christmas-tree filling stations.

"Funny," she said after minutes of silence between the three of us. "Funny that you came here to make pressure on Ring, fake something to use against him, and all the time he had his own private bomb ticking away in the front of his office. Betty Parker in her neat suits, answering the phone, typing briefs, slowly building up to the explosion point."

"I wonder how many other bombs there are like that in other offices," I said.

"Ring is like any other man," she said slowly, "or maybe just most men. He maybe thinks a lot about the women around him, but he's not the one who makes the move. I guess he's afraid to take the risk of seeming clumsy or eager. He waits — and a woman eventually learns to distrust the man who waits. Betty must have made the first move."

"None of the three of us are real qualified to criticize this Betty — or Mr. Black," said Ann. "Not any of us."

Nile lit another cigarette. "I've got an idea that by tomorrow the old business will be working — Ringling Black shot himself by accident. You, Ann, were just a client. There wasn't any robbery. Ring was cleaning a revolver and — bang! Then Betty Parker will take a trip to visit friends in the East. Ring Black will go East on business, and maybe they'll come back as a family, or maybe they'll settle someplace else. Everybody in Orange County will know about the whole thing, everybody will talk about it for a week or so, and that will be that. I never saw a scandal yet that money and social prestige couldn't cover like a blanket of roses."

"Are we still your prisoners?" I asked.

"Of course not. Nobody's filed a complaint against either of you as far as I know, and I've forgotten everything Miss Field told me. You won't have to knock me out again and make your desperate getaway." Nile seemed easier, her tenseness was gone.

"I've got a pretty good idea that I'm a long ways from being clean," I said.

"Something else, Bill?"

"A big wheel, fellow named Roger Mooney, told me I'd either be a good boy or get the book thrown at me. I'm not being their good boy."

"What can they do to you?"

"Enough. I must have been stupid, but I damn well see it now. As soon as a man gets to be a useful fixer, the people he works for make sure they've got a collar on him. For their own protection — because a fixer gets to know too much. I've been thinking I was just careless and foolish; checks, debts, a forged affidavit, some other stuff, enough for a couple of five-year sentences, maybe more, and all cold, all right there ready to use against me. But I've got a little smarter, and I see now that they put the collar on me deliberately."

Nile rounded a long curve. The lights of downtown Los Angeles were a low, bright ribbon ahead of us. "Is it really bad, Bill?"

I spoke slowly. "It's really bad. I've got it coming, so I'll have to take it. Right now it doesn't sound too real — but tomorrow it will be real. I'm not kidding myself."

"I'm pretty much in the dark about all of that, Bill. Tell me about it."

"For the last three, four years, I've been strictly the smart boy who got favors for important people, mostly clients of the advertising agency I was supposed to work for, but other big people too.

"Sometimes it was little favors — tickets for the Rose Bowl game, that kind of stuff. Sometimes it was just setting up a party, calling a lot of girls, getting some TV or movie stars to come.

"But every now and then something would come up that was mean and nasty. Blackmail, mostly — blackmail is the biggest criminal industry in Southern California. Any newspaperman or smart cop will tell you that. Some client or friend of a client would get his tail in a lawn mower and I'd scrounge around getting it out. Dirty stuff. I've paid bribes to people, slugged a few, done some counter-blackmail.

"So I don't have a friend — Bill Oxford, the guy with a million friends. I forgot what the word 'love' meant in relationship to a woman. And I wore a collar with a good strong chain on it.

"Today I got tired of it. We're not driving to the studio now because I'm so damn interested in good government. It's my way of breaking clean. That's all."

"I understand, Bill. Other things happen in Orange County beside growing oranges and pumping oil. I've seen a lot, too."

"But the collar and chain are still there, Nile. It's going to be rough."

"Is it worth it, Bill? I don't mean breaking clean — but why not be easy on yourself? You've got Ring's stuff. You're too beat up to go in front of a television camera. Why not make a deal, Bill?"

Nile spoke softly, and I was remembering the time around dawn this morning. We'd made a lot of dream plans then.

"Supposing they stop you tonight, Bill? These

hoodlums stop you, or you're arrested as you enter the studio. If they've got warrants out for you, these men you're trying to fight now will see that the police are there waiting for you."

"I'm figuring on that, Nile, and trying to figure around it."

"Why not be smart, Bill?" Now there was a taut, growing desperation in her voice. "I know what happens to a man when the machinery of the law clamps on him and begins to grind him up. I've sent men to San Quentin and to Folsom. What would years in prison do to you, Bill?"

"I know, Nile. But these other years have their own kind of destruction. I've made my choice."

"Maybe you don't feel love for me now, Bill, but we're not done with each other. We're only beginning to find out what we can mean to each other. There is a real Nile Lisbon, Bill, a girl you don't even know yet. She's different — loyal, and she has so much to give — so much — "

"Since I'm not your prisoner any more you can drop me anywhere," said Ann. "I don't have much to give, except what I've been giving on the town. You two are so damn wonderful and fine that I know I'm in the wrong crowd, and it won't be a crowd when I get the hell out. Let me off along here, please."

"Ann," I said, "I'm sorry. Stay with us. You don't have your clothes, or money, or — "

We were headed west on the Hollywood freeway. Nile cut in as though neither Ann nor I had spoken.

"Make up your mind, Bill. I'll be honest — I need you. You're the man. We've only known each other for a single day. Give us a chance. Bill. Don't smash your life now. Make a deal, Bill. You can make a deal."

Pilgrim's Progress. The studio with the waiting television cameras was kind of symbol to me, there in the car racing toward it. I'd been running a crazy obstacle course all day and I was getting close to the end of the thing.

Don't kid yourself either way, Oxford. This is Nile Lisbon beside you. She talks about love, and you've got an idea of what Nile Lisbon can give in living to a man she loves. A good life, a life with meaning to it.

Why throw it away? You don't have a ghost of a chance to do the Ringling Black TV expose, you know that. If some of D'Arcy's troopers don't get to you outside, there'll be a big cop on the inside with a ticket to Quentin for you. You don't know what to say in front of the TV camera and you can't just stand there waving papers and photostats around. They'd cut you off. Some clown with his face banged up and swollen, his clothes torn and dirty. A clown.

"I'd rather see you die trying than quit," said Ann. "I'd die with you if it would help — but don't make a deal."

"Where do you want to get out, Miss Field?" asked Nile, slowing the car as we approached an outlet from the freeway.

"Unless I'm thrown out, I'm not getting out."

"Bill, I'm going to stop near here and you phone."

"Phone whom?"

"Anybody that you can make a deal with. I won't take you to that studio. If you get there it would be the end for you. You can't make the telecast, you know that, and if you even try, these men you say have a collar and chain on you will ruin you. A gesture isn't worth years in prison, Bill. I can't let you do it."

She flipped off the red spotlight and the siren.

"Nile I've got to try it. I'm going to try it."

"Good man," said Ann.

"You are too important to me, Bill. I can't let you do it." Nile cut the wheels into a sharp U turn and headed back to the access road for the freeway.

"What are you doing, Nile?"

"I'm heading the other way. You aren't going to that studio, you aren't going to throw away your life for damn-fool reasons. I need you and I'm not going to lose you!"

"Let's get out, Bill, and take a cab," said Ann as the car swung around a corner.

Point of decision. Nile Lisbon was right in everything she said. Going to the studio was only a gesture, and a gesture that couldn't win. The fifty million dollars would win, the candidate would win, the people of California would hurt a little without realizing it, Oxford would be a number behind a wall, Ann would be a cheapening hustler on a one-way downgrade, and Nile Lisbon would sit on a bar stool, her eyes on some other stranger, appraising, wondering.

"Stop the car, Nile. I'm getting out."

"No!"

I reached for the ignition and Nile jammed on the gas, the car roaring into the eastbound channel of the freeway, the cars around blasting their horns in protest.

Now it was too late to pull the ignition keys and stop the car. Nile was doing nearly sixty and the eastbound freeway was a moving river of cars. A sudden stop now might pile up half a dozen cars in a rolling ripping mass of metal and flesh.

"You bitch!" screamed Ann.

"I'm trying to save a man, not destroy him," said

Nile, her voice still soft and even.

"I've got to live my life my way, Nile. Don't try to force me."

"Why not? Do you and I live by different rules?"

"O.K., Nile, if it's got to be this way." I put my left arm around her neck, my right hand on the wheel. Around us, front, sides, rear, was the river of moving steel.

With my left arm I pulled Nile's head back, with my right hand I fought her two hands for control of the wheel. The car began to lurch a little, still inside its lane of traffic but beginning to swing.

My arm was under Nile's chin and she grabbed at my wrist with her left hand, her nails stabbing into my skin. I saw an opening and eased the car into the next lane. Blood was warm on my wrist as Nile's nails cut deeper, but her head was far back and she didn't dare fight my hand on the wheel because she could not see the road.

There was an outlet road two hundred yards ahead. Nile pressed her foot hard against the gas pedal and we were moving up on the car ahead much too fast. I kicked her foot off the pedal and the car bucked, lurching to the left. There was a wild blare of horns behind us.

"Look out, Bill!" Ann screamed, and I swung out of the way of a Cadillac that was nearly forced into a side swipe.

"Nile! This is insane!" The nails slashed at my wrist and her foot found the pedal again.

We were at the outlet road and I pulled the wheel over, as Nile's right hand fought to keep it straight. Tires screeched and the car lurched as we made the turn.

Floodlights brightened the next turn to the side street — a narrow, sharp curve.

"Brakes! Brakes!" I yelled. We hit the curve much too fast to make it.

The car began to career and I straightened the wheel. We went through low wood fence, our bodies thrown upward. I held Nile tightly. Ann threw her body across mine as we hit the seat again. My right hand was hard on the wheel and the car bounced across a sloping parkway of grass, still straight.

We went across a sidewalk, between two parked cars, and into a street, jamming to a stop against a high curb. We were thrown against the wheel and dash, but not badly.

"Did we all get killed?" asked Ann, lifting herself. "Her, anyway, I hope?"

I took my arm from Nile. "Are you all right?"

"I guess so. That was pretty insane, Bill."

"We could have killed a dozen people."

"All right, Bill Oxford," said Nile. "You made your point. I can't force you. I should have known better than to try."

"Now let's get to the studio, Nile." I looked at my watch. "We've still got better than thirty minutes."

"I'm kind of shaky."

"I'll drive."

"Bill, maybe I'm crazy enough to try all the wrong things, but you know I'm right. Phone somebody, make a deal. Not for me, for yourself. Forget me, if you want to — but don't try to do something that can't help you or anybody else, and that will ruin you."

"I've got to do it, Nile. At least I've got to try with every damn thing I've got."

"Then do it by yourself, you damn fool!" Nile pulled

out the keys and threw them into the darkness. I didn't hear them fall.

Ann opened the door and got out. The car was still nosed in to the curb. I slipped away from Nile and got out. A new set of aches popped out of my muscles as I stood up. I started looking for the keys, wiping blood away from the deep scratches on my wrist.

The keys had fallen somewhere in a tangle of weeds in front of an old house. Ann came over to me, got down on her knees, and began to feel through the weeds.

"We'd better take a cab, Bill."

"Let's try to find the keys first. We can't leave that car sticking out into the street. Somebody'd crash into it."

"That woman — "

"She's playing it the way she sees it, Ann. Playing it hard. Don't blame her for that."

Nile was still in the car. Ann and I were on our knees in the weeds.

"I don't blame her. I damn well respect her, Bill. At least she knows what she wants and fights to get it. I never fought. That's why I respect her. And I hate her!"

The weeds were dry husks. I flicked on my lighter and we bent over, heads close together.

"Maybe she's right, Bill. Everything she says makes sense."

My fingers touched metal. A beer-bottle top among the dry, dusty weeds.

"She's right. Make your deal. Don't smash your head against the wall. Be smart, Bill, be smart. She's right, damn her lousy soul!"

Ann was talking in a low voice, not bitter, but almost

musical with emotion, vibrant.

"And she's a woman, a real one, not half living or washed out like most women. So she's slept around. At least she was looking for something, and that's more than I can say. Make the deal and take her, Bill. Be smart."

I found the keys and took them to Nile.

"Back your car away from the curb, Nile. I'm taking a cab."

I turned away and began to walk, the leather envelope in my hand.

Two women called to me, "Bill!" Nile's voice and Ann's. I walked along the night-black street alone.

CHAPTER EIGHTEEN

It was good to be alone. I moved with long, quick steps, disregarding the aches and bruises. My watch showed eight-thirty. In thirty-five minutes Studio D would be ready and waiting.

This was an old and lonely part of Los Angeles, east of Hollywood. I was looking for either a cruising cab or a phone booth where I could call one. I walked down one long block, with the rustle of the palm fronds on the old trees for company, turning on the next, and only another long, lonely block ahead.

I wondered what Nile and Ann were doing. They hadn't followed me. Somehow I knew when I left them that they would not. What I was going to do had to be done by me alone.

Another long block, and at the end of it was a business street. One filling station, closed and dark, with the phone inside.

A secondhand furniture shop, closed. Two stores, empty, the "For Rent" signs tattered and peeling back from the dirty windows. A small bakery, locked and dark. At the corner a beer-and-wine barroom.

Three old men and an old woman sat at the plywood bar, all of them with glasses of wine in front of them. Behind the bar was another old man, his neck thin and wattled like a turkey's. He was wearing a dirty striped shirt, open at the collar.

All four of them had turned their heads to look at me as I came in, with the aged bartender staring behind the burned and ring-marked plywood. They kept staring, three toothless mouths open, two clamped tight on thin, purple-white lips.

"Yeah?" said the bartender.

"Phone?"

"Nah."

"Any phone near here?"

Five pairs of eyes stared at me, three mouths were open, two were closed. I turned and walked out.

Across the street was a storage-and-van warehouse, closed. Here were the lees of Los Angeles, endless blocks of dying houses, dying people, the years gone, the dreams gone.

Another block without an open store. A few cars passed on the street, no cabs. The hands of my watch pointed to eight-forty. This was silly, watching the minutes slide away when I was only a couple of miles from the television studio.

Another saloon, this one with a license for hard liquor. A jukebox was sobbing hoarsely. I went in. A big fat bartender with a face that had collapsed into drooping flesh, and a single customer, a woman.

"Got a phone?"

The bartender reached under the plank, lifted out a cradle phone, and set it on the bar. I dialed the number of a cab company, gave the cab dispatcher the address, and hung up. The bartender put the phone back under the bar.

I put a dime on the scratched varnish, he pushed it back.

"S'O.K."

"I'll have a straight shot, sour-mash bond, water back."

He shook his head.

"Anything you've got will be O.K."

He put his hand under the bar, pulled out a bottle, poured me a drink.

"I could stand one, honey," said the woman. Thirty-something, blonde, thin, with a green sweater stretched into the shape of two good-sized, sharp-ended funnels sticking out from her chest. I couldn't help thinking of the small, empty sacks that were probably hidden beneath those proud cloth and wire funnels.

"Sure." I pushed out a dollar. The barman took it and poured a highball for her.

"Howja get hurt, honey?"

"Fight."

"Jeez, too bad. Howza other guy?"

"In a hospital."

"Here's how, honey." The highball fell through a trap door in her throat. She arched her back and the funnels stuck out a bit farther. I put another dollar on the bar.

"Jeez, you're a sport. A slugger and a sport that's the kind of guy I'm crazy about, honey."

The bartender poured her another highball.

"You're a stranger around here, aren't you, honey?"

"Yeah."

"This place gets pretty lively after a while. Y'oughta stick around. Lotsa fun."

"I've got a cab coming." Eight-forty-five.

"Aw, tell the driver it was a mistake or sumpin. Stick around. I don't happen to have a date tonight, honey." The highball dropped through the trap and she looked at me expectantly. The bartender looked at the half dollar I had as change, his small oyster eyes lost in the fallen flesh around them. There was a campaign poster behind the bar for the candidate I hoped to destroy.

I picked up the half dollar and they both looked at me like hurt children, old, worn, but still hurt children.

Eight forty-six. I put the half back, nodded.

"Jeez, thanks, sport. I bet you think I'm a real lush."

I shrugged.

"He tells me I'm a drunken old bag. He's my husband," she said, pointing to the fat man with the oyster eyes and the fallen face. "But I don't let him cramp my style none. I have plenty dates and I do plenty on those dates. My name's Lana. What's yours, sport?"

"Sport."

"Yah!"

My cab bleated a horn outside. I went to the door.

"Smart son-of-a-bitch, arencha?" said Lana, and then she yelled a few of the old, dirty, tired words. Ann at thirty-five? And then, years later, in the other place, drinking wine?

The cab driver looked at me.

"Didja get in a fight in that joint, huh?"

"No."

"You sure got in one someplace. You ain't broke?"

"No. The Rockwood television studios on Vine near Sunset. Fast as you can."

"O.K., boss."

Eight-forty-eight.

We cut over to Sunset, past Vermont, Western, and then to Vine. I got out, gave him a dollar and some quarters. Eight-fifty-four.

I walked toward the glass doors of the studio entrance, the leather envelope in my hand. Beyond the doors, along the wide sidewalk, was a waiting crowd of a couple of hundred people, herded into two wavering lines by studio ushers. They were probably waiting for the nine-thirty show, "Be an Idiot," one of the practical-joke TV programs.

"Hey, Oxford!"

Oh-oh. I started for the doors. An usher was looking at me without pleasure. The two men came up from behind me, one on either side.

"It's Oxford. I've seen him around."

Each man had me by an arm. The usher watched us, bright eyes narrowing. I started to pull away from the men.

"There won't be any rough stuff, Oxford," said the man on my right. "We won't take that envelope away from you or anything like that. But you won't make that little speech tonight."

I glanced at him. No detective; one of Whitey D'Arcy's troopers.

"You know why you won't make it?"

"Why?"

"Because if you do, Whitey says he will take care of you personally. Maybe not tomorrow, maybe not next week — but it's a promise. Got it?" They dropped my arms. The usher continued to stare.

"Whitey called from Balboa. He told us to watch this place, and if you came, just to tell you not to make that speech. If you do, he says to tell you, he will make you cry. Maybe that sounds like a big joke, a man crying. It ain't no joke. I've seen Whitey do it. Now you know."

"To us, this is no matter of our concern," said the other man. "We're doing Whitey a favor, passing on what he said."

Eight-fifty-six. I pushed open the glass door and the usher walked toward me.

"Can I help you?" The usher was in front of me, blocking me, and he looked at me without respect or affection. He didn't approve of the way I looked.

"Studio D, please. I'm due there now."

"You are?"

"Right now. Let's go."

He didn't move. "Do you have a studio pass?"

"I'm substituting for Ringling Black in Studio D at nine-five."

"You have to have a pass."

Eight-fifty-seven by the big clock on the wall.

I could slug this bright-eyed monkey in his West Point cadet uniform, and if I did, a jillion more monkeys would pop out of the walls and hustle me off. I might fight D'Arcy and his organization, but I couldn't fight the organization of the Rockwood television network.

"Call the studio's program manager. He knows I'm coming. I'm Bill Oxford of the — "

"You are Mr. William Oxford?"

"That's right."

"I'm sorry, but your — that is, your former agency

has notified the desk here that you are not in their employ, and you are to get no agency courtesies."

Efficient, thorough Roger Mooney! He had called his secretary, she had told her assistant, and the assistant had spent the afternoon letting everybody know that Bill Oxford was out in the lonely cold.

I started to laugh and it hurt my bruised jaw. Fighting King, racing through the night with Nile behind the siren and the red spotlight, risking a sixty-mile-an-hour smash on the Hollywood freeway, walking through the night in a sprawling slum, daring Whitey D'Arcy, everything — all to be stopped by a studio usher.

"I'm sorry, sir, but people aren't permitted to stand in this lobby."

"Call the program manager."

"What should I tell him?"

"Tell him that the man who's replacing Ringling Black in Studio D is waiting in here while a jerk in a monkey suit — Oh, hell! Just call him!"

In spite of everything, I must still have had some of the old appearance of being a wheel. The kid went to a phone at the desk and made the call.

Eight-fifty-nine. I still had six minutes.

Maybe.

The junior General MacArthur trotted back from the phone.

"I'm sorry, sir. You should have had a studio pass. Follow me, please, sir."

We walked quickly past the grilled chromium gate, along the hushed corridors with the illuminated mural walls, into a silent elevator operated by one of the tiniest and prettiest redheaded girls I have ever seen.

"Studio D," said the natural-born second lieutenant

who was escorting me.

"Right," said the redhead, turning her head to look at my face. She winked and her pretty, smiling mouth curved around an O.

The elevator stopped, she swung back the sliding door, and said, "Studio D," as ladylike a beautiful small redhead as you can imagine.

We stepped out on the deep, soft gray carpet of the ante-room to three of the smaller TV stages. The door oozed closed behind us.

The lad in the monkey suit walked ahead of me. A man sitting in a deep, soft chair of yellow fuzz turned to see us, and waved at me. It was Roger Mooney.

"I had kind of a hunch you might turn up here, Oxford. I almost had my secretary call the Hollywood station and have them send over a couple of officers to pick you up."

"Good evening, Mr. Mooney," chirped the boy wonder in the monkey suit.

I was looking at the door beyond Mooney, the door marked D. The clock on the far wall showed one minute after nine. Mooney's eyes were on the leather envelope.

"Do you think they'd dare let you get in front of a TV camera looking as you do?" asked Mooney. "Oxford, the agency is on the spot here. We've got too much to lose!"

The usher faded away.

I started to go past Mooney toward D. Mooney stood up, put a hand on my arm.

"If you go in that door, Oxford, you'll regret it until you die."

"People have been telling me that all evening."

"Bill, we can make a deal. If you haven't been happy

at the agency, if your salary should be adjusted upward, or maybe a bonus — "

"No."

He held my arm. His face was red, the blue eyes bulging, and he breathed in puffs.

"What's your interest in this, Bill? Are you a do-gooder all of a sudden? Does it really matter to you who's nominated in this primary election?"

"Not too much. There are plenty of good men in office from California, and personally I'd hate to see a rat like this character get in. But that's not the reason I came here."

Two minutes after nine.

"What is the reason, then, Bill? You know what you're throwing away — "

"That's why I'm here. To throw all that away. I'm starved for a little decency, a little respect from other men that I've earned by doing a job. Maybe I'm crazy, but that's what I want, and that's why I'm here."

"You've always had respect, Bill. We've all liked you at the agency. How many young men your age make the money you do?" He wiped at his forehead, but the sweat oozed.

"How many are as deep in debt as I am? How many of them get jobs like going to Balboa and using any dirty means possible to frame a man because he's trying to be a decent citizen?"

"You're excited, Bill." The red flush of his face was fading into pale white.

"Damn right I'm excited. In three minutes I'm going to stand in front of those cameras and read the stuff in this envelope, show the photostats to maybe a million people. They're going to see my face and my torn clothes — but they'll see the stuff you and the big shots and D'Arcy and the whole rotten gang of you tried to stop. They're going to see it because for once Bill Oxford wasn't bribed, bluffed, or scared. For once I'm not soft and rotten!"

"Next you'll be going to church." Mooney was in a rage, his neck arteries swollen.

"That figures too. Maybe I will. Maybe a church has got something I need."

I pushed his arm away and started for the door marked D.

"Bill — "

His voice was different. I stopped and turned.

He was smiling, his teeth together in a grin like King McCarthy's when he was going into a fight. He was smiling, terribly, his eyes staring and his right hand digging at his shirt over his heart. I tried to get to him before he fell, but he toppled forward, a slender little man whose blue eyes were frozen now, whose fifty-thousand-dollar-a-year heart had finally ripped.

His body was light, easy to turn over so that he rested more easily. I pulled the cushion from the yellow fuzz chair and put it under his legs, trying to ease the strain on his heart. Then I ran to the elevator and pushed the button.

The door slid back and the pretty redhead looked at me.

"Get some help, quick. Roger Mooney's had a heart attack!"

I went back to him, knelt there, and waited. By the time ushers and the studio doctor arrived it was six minutes after nine and Roger Mooney was dead.

But he'd really died with his boots on, trying.

CHAPTER NINETEEN

They were taking the husk of Roger Mooney away, and I went to the door marked D. It was locked.

I stood there, the leather envelope under my arm, tugging at the door. On the far wall the hands of the clock glided to nine-seven. Foolish, crazy, the whole thing. The door was locked.

"Pardon me, sir."

I turned around and saw the usher.

"I'm sorry, but I made a mistake, sir." He looked as smug and smooth as he ever had before, mistake or no mistake. "You were scheduled for the stage here, but the program manager had already canceled you out."

"But you talked to him less than ten minutes ago!"

"Oh, no, sir. I talked to his assistant's secretary. I would never call the program manager directly myself, sir. Never."

"I see."

"Miss Sislain didn't know of the cancellation when I called. This stage is locked, sir."

"Yeah." I felt like an empty bottle.

"Would you care to see the assistant program manager, sir? He'll be free for five minutes at nine-forty-five."

"No, just give him my best." I started toward the elevator.

"How come Mr. Mooney didn't know of the cancellation? He was waiting for me here."

"I believe the cancellation was very sudden, sir. About twenty minutes ago."

"Who the hell canceled it?"

"You would have to see the assistant program manager, sir. At nine-forty-five."

"Yeah. It won't be necessary."

I found a stairway, walked down. The usher followed me like a watchdog.

At the foot of the stairs there was a twenty-four-inch screen in a bone-white console. I glanced at it. Some dreamy-eyed lad in a white turban was playing piano and staring at the video audience with calf eyes, presumably loaded with sex. It was apparent that he thought they were. This must be the emergency relief.

The usher was still with me and he led me to the big room with the glass doors.

Nile and Ann were there together, talking to another usher. I went up to them, but I didn't want to see either of them. I didn't want to see anybody.

"What happened, Bill?" one of them asked the question, I don't know which one.

"I didn't make it. I got here on time, but I had been canceled out a little while before. I don't know why. Somebody with lots of moxie, I suppose, put the pressure on."

"Bill, I'm so sorry." I wasn't looking them; I was looking away, at the big clock that pointed to nine-fifteen. My brief bout with glory would have been over by now.

"Let's all go somewhere and get drunk," I said. "I know just the place, too. It's over east. A girl named Lana told me the place is really fine along about now."

"Let's all go somewhere and eat," said Nile.

She looked at me with friendliness, the dark eyes softer and deeper than I had ever seen them before. I felt that she was seeing me as a different kind of man, one who had strength and not weakness, who was defeated and still was strong. I hope I felt like that.

"I've been trying to talk to Ann," Nile said. "I'd like to have her for a friend, not an enemy." She turned toward Ann with an appealing smile.

"You can talk to me," Ann said.

Nile turned to me. "I told her that — that the kind of girl who could go to Black's office with a gun — for a man she hadn't seen in two years — "

"We don't understand each other," Ann said, "but it seems maybe we do have some of the same ideas about men. Some of the same ideas."

"You know what I want to do right now?"

Both women glanced up at me.

"I want to eat. A steak."

"With those bruises on your face?" asked Ann.

"A damned tender steak." I tried to smile. "Probably by tomorrow morning I'll be eating jailhouse mush. Tonight I still want to go first class."

"You earned it," said Ann.

We went outside and we all slid into the front seat of Nile's car.

"Where?" asked Nile.

I didn't answer right away. "I wonder who had the power to cancel that program."

"It doesn't matter now, does it?" Nile whirred the starter.

"Only in what a guy with that kind of power can do to me. Will do."

"You're tough, Bill," said Ann. "I'll bet on you."

"Musso and Frank's on the Boulevard? Some place on La Cienega?" asked Nile.

Ann wasn't trying to keep my morale up. She had said what she believed.

"None of those places. I've known them for a long time, but I won't see much of them any more," I said. "There's a little place downtown — Goodfellow's Grotto. I used to go there when I was on the paper, when I first came here."

"I know where it is." Nile turned off Sunset and headed toward the freeway back to downtown Los Angeles.

I said, "My car's in the parking lot near the Rendezvous, Ann. You might as well go down there and drive around for a few weeks — until the finance company picks it up."

"We talk after the steaks," said Ann.

Goodfellow's Grotto is old, and not fancy. Curtained booths, waiters who have been there a quarter century and more, good food. We were led back to a booth with a simple table, and minutes later we had our steaks. Nobody had a drink.

The coffee was fine. Somehow I began to feel good, although I had to remember my fight with King every time I had a bit of steak.

"How about finding a doctor and getting fixed up, Bill?"

"I'll work out of it. Maybe the best thing we can do is to go back to Balboa. One more night of freedom, maybe some drinks with you, and then a long, warm bath. It sounds a lot better than the Hollywood police station for tonight."

Nile looked at Ann with that appealing smile.

"Ann can stay at my place tonight. Nobody's likely to drop by," she said, with a fragile edge of irony. "My friends seem to be in the Santa Ana Hospital. But you belong in your room in bed, as soon as we can get you there."

"Are the police apt to pick you up at your room in Balboa?" asked Ann. It was hard to tell whether this was her answer to Nile's invitation, or whether she was simply ignoring it.

"I can get Bill one good night's sleep, at least," said Nile. "I'll phone the Newport police from the car and tell them to hold up any action against Bill until later."

"It must be fun to be a district attorney," said Ann.

"Assistant. And it isn't fun, it's a job. It's interesting, but not fun."

The good mood was with me as we drank our coffee. I had failed, but I had tried. I had tested myself and the test had come out right. Let them throw their book at me — I could take it. Ringling Black would understand that at least I had reached the door of Studio D before nine-five with the leather envelope in my hand.

It was back on the front seat of Nile's car in the lot next to Goodfellow's. I wondered how much power it still had. Probably none, not if somebody could cancel out the telecast at the last moment.

I looked at the two women. Ann Field, used as a tool by Harry Podden, but going to Ringling Black with a gun. Everything to lose, nothing to gain, except to help a man. She had gone twice to that office, and the first time was also with everything to lose and nothing to gain except a fragment of self-respect. Pretty good woman, Ann.

Nile Lisbon, her framework of life shattered within one day. She had brought King McCarthy to disaster because she had to know if Bill Oxford would win in a fight without mercy. Ringling Black, whom she would have married in desperation, wounded by Betty Parker, to whom that marriage brought desperation.

Nile Lisbon, at last content with a man, and now about to lose that man to the gray walls of San Quentin. Violent, storm-ridden, but a pretty good woman, Nile.

"Bill, one question, please."

"Yes, Ann?"

"Have you lost the will to fight you had back there on the beach in Balboa? You were going to put across the big fix tonight, the last one, the fix to save yourself. Have you quit?"

Both women were looking across the table toward me.

"No. I haven't quit."

I pushed back my chair. "I didn't tell you before, but one of the things that happened tonight was that my ex-boss, Roger Mooney, died of a heart attack outside the studio door. He died trying to talk me out of the telecast — and it had already been canceled. Neither one of us knew that. It was somebody bigger than Mooney that stopped the telecast. I'm going to find who that is."

"You'll never quit, will you, Bill?" said Ann.

We looked into each other's eyes, Ann and I. For the first time I realized how much alike we were.

"I'm going to telephone. Be right back." I pushed the booth curtain aside and went to the phone on the wall near the small bar of Goodfellow's, the bar for the newspapermen of Los Angeles.

The big man had said he was having a party tonight. They'd probably be having a lot of fun at that party, and those who knew the story would be laughing at Bill Oxford, the smart fixer who turned and tried to fight the big men. The ex-fixer who found the door was locked and the warrants were out. The chump.

The dime clicked into the slot and I dialed the private number.

Hariguchi, the big man's number-one houseboy, answered. I asked for the big man.

"Yes?" It was the big man.

"This is Bill Oxford."

CHAPTER TWENTY

His voice was thick and heavy, tired. "You cost us a lot of money tonight, Oxford. I don't know what you were trying to prove, but damn your soul to hell, you proved it!"

I waited. Things must have been happening fast tonight while Nile, Ann, and I had come up from Newport.

"What are you going to stick us for?" I recognized the tone of his words, the tone of a defeated man. How had he been defeated?

"Oxford? Are you there?"

"Yes, I'm here. You keep talking and I'll listen."

"You crossed us good. Maybe it's just as well — if that yellow dog would act like this under a little pressure, he wouldn't have been much good to us anyway. What I want to know, Oxford, is how much more hell do you intend to raise?"

I knew the answer to that one, even if I didn't know what the big man was talking about. "All the hell that's necessary."

"Here's the deal I'll offer you, Oxford. We've got you and you've got us. We know that. We can smash you and send you to prison. You can get the *News* or some other paper to print those affidavits of Black's and we'll look pretty bad. So let's make a deal."

"Go ahead." I felt as if I were sitting in a big table-stakes poker game where I couldn't see my cards and the other guy was offering to split the pot with me.

"You get the five thousand. We kill those warrants against you. We give you the checks and the rest of the stuff. In return you let us off the hook. If you give that evidence out now, all you can do is hurt us and there's nothing to be gained. Is it a deal?"

"Yes." I split the pot and I had a pile of winnings, but I still didn't know what cards I had in my hands.

"I respect a guy with guts, Oxford. Come to my party and bring some girls."

"I don't know any girls."

"O.K. Where do you want the stuff delivered?"

"The Balboa Inn at Balboa."

"Before noon. Don't cross us, Oxford. We know you've got us."

"It's all right," I said, and hung up.

No San Quentin, no bills, no collar and chain on my neck. What happened? I dropped another dime in the slot and dialed Matt's home.

"Hello, Matt?"

"Is this you, Bill? Bill Oxford?" He sounded warm, friendly, excited a little.

"Right."

"You really scored, kid. Thanks a million for what you did for me. Any time, anything you want — just ask for it."

"I don't know what happened, Matt. I got to the studio and the damn telecast was canceled."

"Sure — the studio newsroom phoned the program director as soon as they got the flash, and naturally the director canceled it. What else?"

"What flash?"

"I'll give you the story. After you phoned me tonight I got to the candidate at his place in Bel Aire. I checked the story you gave me direct with him. He was scared spitless. I stayed there with him and his stooges— every mother's son of them sweating ice cubes — while he lived on the telephone trying to see if you could be stopped. By eight-thirty he decided you couldn't be stopped. You were somewhere, headed for that studio, with evidence that would smash him. At eight-thirty I phoned my paper and the major news services that the lousy punk had withdrawn from the race for nomination because of ill health. It *was* ill health, too he was scared to death. This was a flash bulletin and naturally the Rockwood newsroom passed the bulletin to their program director. He just canceled you out — there wasn't any need for a political telecast.

"Great work, Oxford. I had you all wrong!"

"I just talked to the guy behind the candidate. The ex-candidate. He was real sweet to me, Matt. How come?"

"Hell, you know why Bill. The candidate folded, and now the whole crowd is afraid you'll make them look stupid by giving my paper, or one of the others, the evidence that made him withdraw. You've got the power and they haven't. I don't see any point to it, myself, because you've got the dog out of the race. But you know how they figure — they got whipped tonight, and they've all got their tails between their legs. Good work, Bill!"

"Thanks, Matt."

It was a wonderful night.

I went back to the booth and two women looked at me, dark eyes, gray eyes.

"We won." I told them the story.

There was a change on the way back to Balboa. Nile and Ann were quiet. I talked about things, made jokes, but they didn't say much. Things had changed. Before, I had been a man in trouble, and, however far apart they were in other ways, they had a common interest in trying to help me. Now I wasn't in trouble. I was the man that Nile Lisbon loved and Ann was just a girl, lost and alone. Nile had a career and a man, Ann had the unknown, unfriendly years ahead of her.

It was a little after eleven when we reached Santa Ana to turn off for the Newport Beach road. Nile stopped at the Santa Ana Hospital.

"I'm going in to see how Ringling and King are doing. The staff here know me and they'll let me see them. I won't be long."

She was gone a long time, nearly half an hour.

Ann and I sat there in the front seat of the car in the darkness.

"What are you going to do now, Bill?"

"Get a job. Maybe I can be a newspaperman again. Monday I head for town, and I'll see what Matt can do for me."

"How much does a job like that pay?"

"Around a hundred and eight-five a week. Not bad money."

"What about — about her, Bill?"

"I don't know, Ann. We've known each other only one day, one real rugged day. First I've got to get a job, prove that I can do a regular, honest day's work again. It's going to sound funny, but right now that's more important to me than any woman."

"Are you in love with Nile?"

I thought about that for a while. "Maybe almost any

man can fall in love with Nile Lisbon, Ann."

"Did you?"

"Violently. More than other men, maybe, because both Nile and I were looking for the same thing. I wanted to be a complete man, she needed a complete man. I had to know that she was content with me — the way King and Black were trapped by their need to meet her challenge. Do you understand at all?"

Her voice was soft. "I understand Bill."

"It's changed now. Something that was whipping her is gone. She's at ease with herself, as if she had been climbing a rough, steep hill and somehow now she's reached the top of it."

"She has you."

"I've been wondering if that's it. Maybe not. Coming back from the city I felt that Nile and I have both changed. The terrible, soul-hungry, body-hungry need we had when we met isn't there. I wonder if that was what we thought was love."

"Are you trying to say you don't love Nile?"

"I don't have any answers tonight. But I feel that she and I are different people now than we were this morning. For one thing, that struggle in the car. I wonder if Nile could stay with a man who will fight her and defeat her. I have an idea that John Lisbon maybe wasn't a real strong kind of man; maybe he got his strength from Nile."

"And she's been fooling herself ever since as to the kind of man she really wants and needs?"

"Could be."

"I don't know much about women, Bill, or men. Or anything."

"You know something about Ann Field now."

She was silent for almost a minute. "Yes, I guess I

do. Something good for a change."

We talked about other things until Nile came out from the hospital, pleasant things. Some of the time we laughed, sometimes we were serious.

Nile walked to the car, got in. "I'm sorry I was so long."

"How are they?"

"Ring's fine. He was awake, and we talked a little. As I predicted, Betty will go East to visit friends. There wasn't any robbery, no shooting, just a gun accident. Ring was happy about the candidate. He sent you his best. Naturally he's shaken up. Not by the bullet — he actually seems almost glad that Betty shot him. She's coming to see him in the morning. Is there something different about me, Bill?"

"Maybe."

"Ring and I were different. He was ashamed of things, but not too ashamed, if you know what I mean. And I felt one thing — the infatuation that Ringling had toward me is changed. We're more human together."

We waited.

"Bill, I'll drive you and Ann to Balboa, but then I have to come back here. Two men who have meant very much to me are here, and I've got to come back to — "

"I understand, Nile."

"The thing is — it's hard to explain, but I found out tonight that if I ever found my complete man, the strong man, he wouldn't need me. You don't need me, and I have to have that. I didn't know it until tonight."

"Yes, Nile."

"Ring's world fell in on him this afternoon. And in that other room they've got McCarthy wrapped in bandages, his leg up in a traction splint. In a way I did that to him — not you. There's a lot of repair work I'm going to have to do, and maybe I'd better start on myself."

"Drop us off at Christian's, Nile."

"You belong in bed, not drinking."

"I want a long, cool drink and a lot of laughter around me. That's what I'm going to get."

"You're the man."

She drove us to Newport and the three of us were quiet. I ached and hurt and my clothes felt sticky, but none of that mattered. I didn't have a chain on my neck. It would be fun waking up tomorrow.

"Good-by, Bill. It's been a night of growing up for me, and not easy."

She extended her hand to Ann, and Ann took it.

"Well, good-by, Nile. We don't have much in common — but we both know what hell is, don't we?"

There was a quick deep look. "She's a good one, Bill. It'll work out. We'll see each other?"

"I'm getting a job in town. I'll call you, Nile."

"Good-by Ann. Good-by, Bill."

"Good-by, Nile."

We watched her drive back to Central on the way to the hospital where Black and McCarthy waited for her and needed her. It had been love — a violent night and day of love — and that was it. I had come into her life, found the whirlpool and the typhoon, and we had moved apart, both changed and different.

Ann and I walked past the fancy stuff in front of Christian's, the old pilings, the nets, and the almost tropical little jungle of banana trees and palms. The place seemed to be bursting with light, music, and laughter. This was the first of the nine nights of the rites of spring, and Christian's was crowded.

"I look kind of bad for this place, Ann," I said, "but I don't mind if you don't."

"You look great, Bill."

We walked up the steps and turned toward the crowded bar. I had one last thought about Nile. If she had won out in the struggle in the car, if I had turned back from trying to reach Studio D, we might still be in love.

The tall girl with the red-gold hair who had been sun-bathing on the yacht in the bay yesterday was near the entrance, long sleek legs drawn up on her bar stool. She was talking to a young man and laughing.

Next to her, watching her, was Whitey D'Arcy, and beyond him were two of his men.

Ann and I walked by. D'Arcy looked up, saw me.

"You, Oxford. Did you get my message, boy?"

"I got it."

"And?"

"Stick it."

He looked at me with surprise, and then cold hate.

"You suddenly a hard man, Oxford?"

"That's right." I could feel Ann's fingers clenched on my arm. Whitey's troopers were watching me with amusement, the way cruel boys might look at a dog about to be tortured.

"Very soon, Oxford. Wherever you are and damn soon. Do you ever cry, Oxford?" He smiled and turned away, back to look at the girl with the red-gold hair.

Ann and I got close to the bar. I ordered two long, cool drinks.

"You know what you're doing, Bill?" Ann whispered.

"Yes."

"You'll have to get away from these parts now."

"I'm staying."

"Bill, you can't fight him. You did that in front of his men. He can't let you get away with that."

"I couldn't let him get away with giving me orders, either. It had to be that way, Ann."

"I'm glad, Bill. But I'm scared."

We sipped at our drinks, while the kids talked and laughed around us.

"Hey, fellow!"

I turned around. The boy with the red-haired girl was talking to D'Arcy.

"This girl doesn't want you bothering her. Dig that?"

D'Arcy laughed. "Beat it, punk. I want to talk to this little sugar."

The two troopers had moved forward toward the boy. The girl was looking at D'Arcy, her eyebrows high.

"Get going, kid. And you, baby, you kind of fascinate me. Howsabout it? I'm Whitey D'Arcy."

Everybody was watching now. D'Arcy, his two men, the long-legged girl with the red-gold hair, the boy. The boy looked strong, but he looked young, twenty-two maybe.

"It don't much matter who you are, fellow. Stop bothering this girl." He had a Southern speech, maybe from Arizona or New Mexico.

One of the troopers shoved the boy.

All that Ann and I did was to stay clear. Five, maybe six of the young men moved like a basketball team on the hoodlum. I saw him go down from a professional one to the heart and two to the jaw by the boy he'd shoved.

It was a busy fight while it lasted, which was maybe two minutes.

The barmen from the Hut, along with the manager, who looked unworried and unexcited, pulled the boys off Whitey and his two men. Whitey looked a lot worse than King McCarthy had earlier. They lifted him up, and he was trying to spit teeth through the blood. His nose was a smashed strawberry and his hands were over his ribs as if he didn't have many of them left.

What I noticed most was that he was crying, the tears bubbling out of his closed, swollen eyes, and he was moaning through the wreck of his mouth.

His two men were smashed up as badly as Whitey. The barmen carried the three into a back room, and the young men, none of them showing any wear, went back to their girls. The girl with the red-gold hair had sat on the bar stool the entire time, watching with patient interest.

When the bartender came back and after he had washed his hands, I ordered two more drinks. As he mixed them he shook his head.

"Fellows like that ought to know better than to start trouble in Balboa during Easter week. They'd be better off just staying away from this town. These kids are real great, but they're touchy, and they won't let guys like those fool around with their girls."

He served the drinks and shook his head again.

"Those three birds will be in the hospital for a couple months easy. They got wrecked."

"That was Whitey D'Arcy and two of his hoods," I said.

"Yeah?" He looked interested. "I've read about him. Real tough bird. Well, that was part of the U.S.C. football team he just met."

Ann laughed.

"Of course, none of us will remember who worked

those bums over," the barman continued. "The three bums will get out of the hospital and then they'll be up on a disorderly-conduct warrant. We've got a real cool woman assistant D.A. in this county, name of Mrs. Lisbon. She'll see that the book gets thrown at 'em. We don't scare easy in Orange County."

Whitey D'Arcy and his men beaten up by some college boys and then spending thirty days or so working for the county. I could forget him, too.

Ann and I left the Hut and walked toward the ocean. We could hear the music and the young voices of the nine days of Easter through the night.

The roar of the long combers breaking into the surf was loud and the moon was rising in silver over the sea blackness.

"This is what I wanted to do with you six years ago, Bill. Walk along the dunes and wait for the night to end."

"We can do it now, Ann. It's not too late for us."

THE END

John Donald McPartland was born April 13, 1911, in Chicago, Illinois. In 1943, he was inducted into the U.S. Army, and later, as an Army Reservist, he served again in the Korean War, at which point he became a staff writer on the *Stars and Stripes* newspaper. In between wars, he wrote a book, *Sex in Our Changing World*, and joined the staff of *Life* magazine. After Korea, he moved to Monterey, California, and began to publish a series of hardboiled thrillers with Gold Medal Books. And after his early death in Monterey on September 14, 1958, from a heart attack, it was discovered that he had two families—his legal wife and son in Mill Valley, California; and a mistress in Monterey who bore him five children and was named "Mother of the Year" in 1956.

BLACK GAT BOOKS

Helen Nielsen · The Woman on the Roof #9
Lou Cameron · Angel's Flight #10
Gary Lovisi · The Affair of Lady Westcott's Lost Ruby / The Case of the Unseen Assassin #11
Arnold Hano · The Last Notch #12
Clifton Adams · Never Say No to a Killer #13
Ed Lacy · The Men From the Boys #14
Henry Kane · Frenzy of Evil #15
William Ard · You'll Get Yours #16
Bert & Dolores Hitchens · End of the Line #17
Noël Calef · Frantic #18
Ovid Demaris · The Hoods Take Over #19
Fredric Brown · Madball #20
Louis Malley · Stool Pigeon #21
Frank Kane · The Living End #22
Ferguson Findley · My Old Man's Badge #23
Paul Connolly · Tears are for Angels #24
E. P. Fenwick · Two Names for Death #25
Lorenz Heller · Dead Wrong #26
Robert Martin · Little Sister #27
Calvin Clements · Satan Takes the Helm #28
Jack Karney · Cut Me In #29
George Benet · The Hoodlums #30
Jonathan Craig · So Young, So Wicked #31
Edna Sherry · Tears for Jessie Hewitt #32
William O'Farrell · Repeat Performance #33
Marvin Albert · The Girl With No Place to Hide #34
Edward S. Aarons · Gang Rumble #35
William Fuller · Back Country #36
Robert Silverberg · The Killer #37
William R. Cox · Make My Coffin Strong #38
A. S. Fleischman · Blood Alley #39
Harold R. Daniels · The Girl in 304 #40
William H. Duhart · The Deadly Pay-Off #41
Robert Ames · Awake and Die #42
Charles Runyon · Object of Lust #43
Paul Conant - Dr. Gatskill's Blue Shoes #44
Asa Bordages - Murders in Silk #45
Darwin Teilhet - Take Me As I Am #46
Stephen Marlowe - Blonde Bait #47
Jonathan Latimer - The Fifth Grave #48
Andrew Coburn - Off Duty #49
Basil Heatter - Any Man's Girl #50
Day Keene - Acapulco G.P.O. #51
John P. Browner - Death of a Punk #52
Glenn Canary - The Trailer Park Girls #53
Jacquin Sanders - Freakshow #54
John & Ward Hawkins - The Floods of Fear #55
Richard Jessup - Night Boat to Paris #56
Arnold Drake - The Steel Noose #57
William Vance - Bait #58
Jay Flynn - Drink With the Dead #59
Charles Burgess - The Other Woman #60
Gil Brewer - Wild #61
Thomas B. Dewey - Hunter at Large #62
Martha Albrand - Remembered Anger #63
Conrad Dawn - Chartered Love #64
H. Vernor Dixon - Too Rich to Die #65
Lee Wells - Day of the Outlaw #66
Elliott Gilbert - Vice Trap #67
Emmett McDowell - Switcheroo #68
Louis King - Cornered #69
Wenzell Brown - The Wicked Streets #70
Dana Wilson - Make With the Brains, Pierre #71

www.ingramcontent.com/pod-product-compliance
Lightning Source LLC
Chambersburg PA
CBHW050336160726
48002CB00001B/344

* 9 7 9 8 8 8 6 0 1 1 5 2 4 *